THE HONOUR KILLING

J. S. HAMILTON

Published by

MELROSE BOOKS

An Imprint of Melrose Press Limited
St Thomas Place, Ely
Cambridgeshire
CB7 4GG, UK
www.melrosebooks.co.uk

FIRST EDITION

Copyright © J. S. Hamilton 2017

The Author asserts his moral right to
be identified as the author of this work

Cover by Melrose Books

ISBN   **978-1-912026-74-6 paperback**
         978-1-912026-75-3 epub
         978-1-912026-76-0 mobi

All rights reserved. No part of this publication may be reproduced, stored in a retrieval system, or transmitted, in any form or by any means electronic, mechanical, photocopying, recording or otherwise, without the prior permission of the publishers.

This book is sold subject to the condition that it shall not, by way of trade or otherwise, be lent, re-sold, hired out or otherwise circulated without the publisher's prior consent in any form of binding or cover other than that in which it is published and without a similar condition including this condition being imposed on the subsequent purchaser.

Printed and bound in Great Britain by:
Ashford Colour Press Ltd
Unit 600
Fareham Reach
Fareham Road
Gosport
PO13 0FW

Contents

Index of Names

Mahmood Asgar: *The deceased*
Parveen Ashkani: *Asgar's wife*

Abdul Mahmood: *Parveen's brother*
Rashid Khan: *Parveen's uncle*
Aisha Khan: *Nadeem's wife*
Bakar Abdul: *Asgar's uncle in Oldham*
Tariq Khan: *Asgar's father*

Nadeem Khan:
Wahid Mahmood: } *Brothers of Parveen – accused*

Sam Leonard:
Omar Fazal: } *Accused*
Jack Rastrick:

Asif Khan: *Wahid Mahmood's cellmate*
Saber Malik: *Parveen's friend in Cardiff*
Sandra Jaimes: *Omar Fazal's girlfriend*
Suzanne Leonard: *Sam Leonard's wife*
Helen Munro: *Jack Rastrick's girlfriend*

Detective Superintendent Bob Illingworth:
Detective Inspector James Turnbull:
Detective Sergeant Dave Jasper:
Detective Sergeant John Roberts: *Police*
Detective Jonathan Crawford:
Detective Falkener:
Detective Jane Rowley:

Bill Thornton: *SOCO*
Professor John Talbot: *Pathologist*
Jane Michaels: *Governor of Leeds Prison*
Doormen Incorporated: *Employer of Sam Leonard and Omar Fazal*
John and Jane Abbott: *Witnesses at the scene*
Narinda: *Counsellor*

Tom Beecroft, Q.C.
Mr Oldroyd: *Counsel for the Prosecution*

Miss Davies, Q.C.
Mr Dodds: *Counsel for Nadeem Khan*

Mr Archbold, Q.C.
Miss Wadham: *Counsel for Wahid Mahmood*

Mr May, Q.C.
Miss McLean: *Counsel for Sam Leonard*

Mr Mountfield, Q.C.
Mr Blackstone: *Counsel for Jack Rastrick*

Mr Stewart, Q.C.
Mr Batty: *Counsel for Omar Fazal*

Chapter 1
The Body

John and Jane Abbott were looking forward to watching *Top Gear* on television. It was a typical West Yorkshire Sunday evening in February, dank and miserable, but not yet raining.

It was 8:00 p.m. and the day was drawing in. They were on their way home from a long and heavy Sunday lunch with members of the family at The Goose Inn at Ogden. Their route took them over the moors between Halifax and Bradford. John took this route through fear that, if breathalysed, it would prove positive. He knew the roads well. He loved the moors – wild land divided by irregular dry-stone walls, sheep sheltering in huddles behind and gorse covering the higher ground. It made John think of *Wuthering Heights*; bleak and desolate yet beautiful.

John had loved the area since he was a boy. His dad used to take him, his brothers and their dog over the moors by Ogden Reservoir. Bleak, with heather divided by a well-trodden path down to a stream which led to a small waterfall where they would sit and his dad would enjoy a cigarette. Oh happy days.

As he approached a junction on his left, a remote spot high on the moor, a car suddenly reversed into his path and nearly collided with his near side. He swerved and braked, nearly hitting the wall on his offside. His heart missed a beat and he broke out in a hot sweat. 'Bloody fool,' he explained to Jane. 'And what's he doing there at this time on a grey winter's day? Maybe he's got a girl in there.'

As John passed the junction and swerved, Jane was looking to her left at the car which had nearly hit them.

'John, there was a body in the road.'

'Don't be stupid.'

'No, I swear. I saw it in the headlights.'

John became nervous as the other car had now re-emerged and was close behind him. As he approached another junction, he turned right in the hope that the other car would go straight on. It did – he breathed a sigh of relief.

'Are you sure?'

'Well, it looked like a body.'

'Should we go back?' he asked.

'Yes, of course we should,' replied Jane.

'But we'll then get involved, and if we call the police, I might be breathalysed; and it might be nothing.'

'Figs to that,' said Jane. 'There was a body back there.'

'Alright,' replied John. 'On your head be it.'

He turned around and retraced his route. He turned right into the junction and stopped, putting his headlights on full beam as he did so. There on the road was a person-sized shape lying full length. They got out and approached. It was, as they thought, the body of a man. It was lain face down in a crab-like position. There was no blood visible. His eyes were open in a look of sheer terror and there was an unnatural stillness to the body.

The man was Asian, probably in his early thirties, dressed in shirt and trousers, but no jacket or overcoat.

John felt nauseous, as did Jane who vomited at the roadside. John said, 'I'll call 999 and you do what you can.' Jane had no training in first aid, but put the man into the recovery position, which she had seen on television. He was still breathing and was just able to utter the word "Joe".

They waited anxiously – the man did not stir. Twenty minutes later, the ambulance arrived with its blue lights flashing. 'We'd trouble finding you,' said one of the paramedics as he proceeded to examine the body. 'He's still breathing. He's been shot in the back; he looks bad, so no promises.' They put him in the ambulance and rushed him to Halifax General Infirmary.

The A&E Department was busy. It was always thus on a Sunday night. Full of drug over-dosers and drunks with minor injuries.

The man was rushed past waiting patients into the Emergency Room where his clothes were cut off. The A&E team found two bullet wounds in his back and one in his right leg.

Emergency resuscitation began. One bullet was removed from his right lung and one from his right leg. No further surgery was attempted because of his serious condition.

At 4:00 a.m. the man's heart stopped beating and he was pronounced dead.

Chapter 2
The Murder Scene

By chance, Detective Jonny Crawford was driving in the opposite direction to the Abbotts. He was off duty and was driving home to Halifax after a monotonous Sunday in the Bradford C.I.D. office doing paperwork; always stashes of paperwork much of which, to him, seemed pointless. He liked this route between Thornton and Halifax for its beauty and it was a challenge for his driving skills. He saw the car, which later was to cause the Abbotts to swerve, stationary in the junction. *What on earth could they be doing*, he thought, *what an odd place to stop, right on top of the moor, at this time on a winter's day.*

He, ever observant, saw two men in the car. Always a policeman, he made – as was his habit – a mental note that the car looked like a Peugeot 405 or a Rover 414, beige in colour and the old model, and that the men appeared to be in their twenties or thirties. As far as he could tell, in the fading light, they were white.

He noticed that the car boot was open and a third man was standing by the driver's door. The car was facing inwards. This man, he thought, was about 5' 9" tall, white and in his thirties. He was wearing a workman's yellow fluorescent jacket which covered his arms. Crawford wondered if he should stop, but as he was now off duty, tired and it was cold, he continued on his way home.

'I'm sure it was nothing,' he said to himself – more in hope than expectation. He turned out to be very wrong.

Chapter 3

The Investigation

Detective Inspector James Turnbull of the West Yorkshire Homicide Crime Unit, based in Bradford, was also looking forward to a peaceful Sunday night at home in Idle, Bradford, with his wife, Helen.

He was listening to Classic FM playing Bach's "Air on a G String", one of his favourite classical pieces. He was sucking on an unlit pipe, his way of trying to stop smoking.

His wife, Helen, was knitting in front of the log burner. He was contented with life. He was fifty-two, not far off retirement but enjoying his work as head of the Bradford Homicide Squad. He was a Bradfordian born and bred. His father had been a policeman before him, ending up as a sergeant in the custody suite in Bradford City Hall, where headquarters was based at that time.

Turnbull had attended the local grammar school and left to join the police force at his earliest opportunity, first as a cadet and then a PC on the beat.

Bradford had changed dramatically during his lifetime from a prosperous city whose wealth relied on the wool trade. Bradford's soft water was perfect for washing wool and the industry grew and grew until the early Fifties.

At its height, Bradford boasted more Rolls Royce cars per capita than anywhere in the UK. The city's shops, Marshall & Snelgrove, Brown & Muffs, Busby's, Fattorini's and many others, were prosperous, a magnet for Bradfordians and those from the outlying districts of Ilkley and Harrogate. Darley Street was populated by a succession of thriving shops, china retailers, jewellers, chemists and tailors.

But then began a gradual decline. The mills were largely privately owned and their owners preferred to sit and chat in the Wool Exchange and the Bradford and Union Club than advance their technology. Investment in modern machinery reduced, and competition from the Far East, with its cheap labour, made Bradford's cloth expensive.

In order to face this competition, the city took in huge numbers of Pakistanis, whose labour was cheap.

His father used to say that he remembered the days when the buildings in Bradford were black and the people were white.

No longer. But times change and Turnbull appreciated the cultural diversity which the city now enjoyed. He loved curries and, on the whole, found the Asian community friendly but remote. The Bradford riots had proved a strain on the community, but things were slowly getting back to normal.

Turnbull's reminiscing was disturbed by the phone ringing.

'Sir, it's Dave.' Detective Sergeant Dave Jasper was Turnbull's sergeant in the crime unit. 'We've reports of a shooting on our patch, on the moors outside Halifax. I can give you the grid reference and the postcode. I'm sorry to disturb you, but I think we should be there.'

'Who's there now?' Turnbull asked.

'The paramedics have taken the injured man to Halifax General. It looks as though he's been shot in the back. There's a uniformed presence and they've cordoned off the crime scene. D.S. Roberts is on his way there with D.C. Thornton.' They were part of the same team and Turnbull was thankful – they were good men.

'Okay,' said Turnbull. 'I'll set off now. Tell them I'm on my way.' He told Helen the bad news.

'Not another …' she said. 'When will you be back?'

'God knows. Don't wait up for me.' This, he reflected, was the third night he'd been called out that week when off duty and, at his rank, he didn't get paid overtime. *Is there any* end *to West Yorkshire's heavy crime?* he thought. As if he didn't have a big enough workload already. Bradford Crown Court lists were awash with murder trials, more than any other court on the North Eastern Circuit. *Let's hope he survives*, he thought. *It could give us a lead, but it doesn't sound hopeful.*

His journey took him into Bradford and out on the Haworth Road, until he reached Queensbury, where he turned on to the minor road leading to the crime scene. He was at the junction in half an hour. The road was some twenty feet wide with stone walls on each side. The tarmac was in good condition. There were no street lights because of the remoteness and it was dark.

By now, Turnbull saw that the scenes of crime officers (SOCO) were at the scene. Searchlights were in place and the road was closed. He saw that the force photographer, Peter Renshaw, was photographing the scene. It had started to drizzle and bursts of the camera's flash caught the drizzle in midair.

The senior SOCO present was Bill Thornton, whom Turnbull knew well. 'Now then, Bill, found anything?' asked Turnbull.

'Yes, so far we have accounted for two bullets and a bullet casing. We think one bullet hit the wall over there and plugged in the road and I've been told that the man who's been taken to hospital has had a bullet removed from his lung and one from his leg.'

'Know who he is?' he asked of his team.

'No, sir,' replied D.S. Roberts. 'He's an Asian, mid-thirties, not dressed to be out on a cold night in a shirt, slacks and slippers. He was shot in the back, it seems at close range. It almost looks like an execution, poor sod.'

Roberts was in his late twenties, wearing a fashionable raincoat. *Hardly suitable,* thought Turnbull.

'Anything on him to help?'

'Maybe,' replied the sergeant. 'He's £30 on him and a leisure card with no name. We're trying to trace the owner through that. We won't be able to get an ID from it until tomorrow morning.'

'It can't have been a robbery otherwise they would have taken the thirty,' stated Turnbull. He thought that the shooting had all the hallmarks of a drug war, but it could also be a family feud. 'We'll have a conference at eight o'clock tomorrow morning. Keep me informed of any developments.'

He spent an hour inspecting the scene and then drove home thinking he had missed *Prime Suspect,* but he'd recorded it. Once home, he sat alone with a scotch and watched the programme. His favourite tipple was Bell's with ice and water. Helen was, by now, in bed and he assumed she would be asleep.

He thought, as he admired Jane Tennyson, *an assassination at close range? "Why?" is the question.* A shooting in the back – it had the hallmarks of an execution. It could be a drugs war. There had been shootings recently in Bradford between Asian gangs who sold drugs, when one encroached on another's patch.

Another possibility was what had become known as an "honour killing". These were prevalent in all Asian communities. There was nothing "honourable" about them – the murder of a member of a family because of family disapproval of a marriage.

When he had been working in London early in his career, he had investigated what turned out to be an "honour killing" where the victim had been wrapped in industrial cellophane and suffocated to death. This murder was perhaps another such case. This would make detection easier than if it was a drug-war killing because honour killings normally pointed to family involvement.

"Honour killings" he knew to be the murder of a family

member who had slighted the "honour" of a family. He knew them to be prevalent in Pakistan where they were considered to be somehow justifiable. The police often turned a blind eye. Here, in England, it was murder – full stop.

He switched channels and watched Jeremy Clarkson testing a Jaguar XJ. *How I'd love one, but fat chance on my pay,* thought Turnbull. He thought further about the killing. It didn't typify a drug war which usually involved multiple shoot-outs. This was private. By his clothing, it looked as though the deceased had been forcibly taken from his home without having time to wrap up against the cold night air.

Conceivably, it could be a racial killing by far right groups, but this didn't bear the usual hallmarks of a racial killing. No daubing of the body or slogans left at the scene.

This was unusual. An execution.

Before long, Turnbull would require an Asian officer in his team who could get under the skin of these Asian killings. At the moment, he felt an outsider.

Whilst work was so busy, Turnbull felt his home life was suffering. He hadn't taken Helen out for ages and, because of his crazy hours, they slept separately most of the time. *Maybe this one will be wrapped up quickly,* he thought, *and then I could take Helen away for a few days.* She always talked of Paris. He would ring Thomas Cook when the case was over. He thought of the galleries, the museums, the dinners in small restaurants on the Left Bank and of Montmartre.

He put on some soothing late-night music on Radio 2. His log burner still had some glowing embers, so he put a log on; it crackled into life, exuding the wonderful smell of burning wood.

He thought about his team. Dave Jasper was a good sergeant whom he may lose soon as he was taking his inspector's exams.

Jon Crawford was not experienced enough to take over. He

was young and married with two young children. Not an easy life for a young detective.

But that, he thought, is the name of the game. At least I have a full team for this investigation, which was likely to be messy.

Chapter 4
The Following Morning

By now, D.C. Jon Crawford had heard of the murder from gossip in the C.I.D. office at Bradford Central and reported to D.I. James Turnbull, in his boss's office, what he had seen. 'Never mind, lad,' said Turnbull. 'We all make mistakes. The secret is to learn from them. At least we know from you that there were three, probably white, killers – one wearing a fluorescent jacket – in a car which looked like a Peugeot 405 or a Rover 414. God knows what would have happened if you had stopped. You could be dead as well.'

Jon felt better about his mistake, but swore to himself that he would never repeat it.

Dave Jasper told Turnbull he was going across to City Hall to identify the holder of the leisure card. They should be open by now, it was 9:00 a.m.

He walked out of headquarters and turned left towards City Hall. He admired the Alhambra Theatre just across the road. It always brought back fond memories of when, as a boy, he went to the pantomimes there.

He crossed over to City Hall and went to the administration office. He showed his warrant card and then the leisure card. 'I need to know who's the holder of this membership card. Can you help me?'

'Sure,' said the blond, fortyish-year-old, helpful Yorkshire woman. 'Wait a minute.' She went across the office to a filing cabinet and came back with a file. 'The holder is shown as one Mahmood Asgar with an additional user, his wife, Parveen Ashkani. His address is shown as 34 Priestley Street, Oldham. Does that help?'

'Perfect. Thanks for your help. Can you copy those membership details for me?'

She returned with a copy and a smile. *Bit old for me,* thought Jasper, and returned to headquarters where he told Turnbull the good news.

'Try and trace whose address that is.'

'Sure,' said Jasper and rang Oldham City Council. 'This is Detective Sergeant Dave Jasper from Bradford C.I.D. We are trying to trace the occupants of 34 Priestley Street, Oldham. Can you help?'

'Hold on and I'll find out for you,' said the lady at the council office. A few minutes later she returned to the phone. 'It's a council property, rented to one Bakar Abdul and his wife Jaleel.'

'Do you know if they're on the phone?'

'No, they're not.'

'Oh well, it was worth a try. Will you email me to say you made this enquiry and why, just for our records? I'll give you our email address.'

'Certainly.'

He thanked her for her help and then told Turnbull of his discovery.

'Okay,' said Turnbull as he turned to Jon Crawford who was sitting nearby. 'Crawford, will you go to Oldham? That'll be a nice trip over the M62.'

Oh, God, thought Jon, he hated the M62. It was always congested.

'Certainly, sir,' Jon replied, hoping he wouldn't make a cock of this.

He set off from Bradford, in an unmarked Ford Escort, on the dreary journey to Oldham down the M606 and onto the M62, heading west which, as usual, was congested. Roadworks soon fouled up his progress. He began to wish he had gone on the old road through Halifax and Huddersfield. Eventually, after an hour and a half, he found the house.

He rang the doorbell and two Asian people answered the door. He introduced himself, produced the necessary identification and was invited in. The two introduced themselves as Bakar Abdul and his wife Jaleel.

'Sorry to disturb you,' Crawford said. 'But we're making enquiries about one Mahmood Asgar. Do you know him?'

'Yes,' Bakar replied. 'He lived here – 'til last week. He's moved to Halifax. I think he's married to a girl called Parveen Ashkani, although we never saw her. He is a relative of ours who came over recently from Pakistan.'

'Thanks,' said Crawford. 'Have you got an address for him so you could forward his mail?'

'Afraid not,' replied Bakar.

Jon thanked them and, on returning to his car, radioed the information to headquarters.

———•◆•◆•◆•———

That same morning, Parveen Ashkani, went to 8 Grove Road in Halifax expecting to find her husband there. He was very secretive. She had left food for him outside the back door the night before, but it was still there. She was worried. She did not have a key to the house and no credit on her mobile phone – what a time for that to happen – so she found a telephone box and called Asgar's number. No reply. She now began to panic and decided to call the police.

As luck would have it, at that moment, a police car passed her. She flagged it down and told the driver, 'I'm worried about my husband. I think something has happened to him. Can you help?' She felt more comfortable because the policeman was Asian.

'Don't worry, love, we'll sort this out. First of all, where does he live?'

'I'll show you,' she said as she got in the car and directed him the short distance to the house.

The policeman thumped on the door repeatedly. No answer. 'Why haven't you got a key?' he asked Parveen.

'The letting agents only gave us one.'

'Well, let's go to them and get the master key.'

He drove a short distance to the letting agents where Parveen explained the situation. 'You remember me? I rented the house for Mahmood Asgar, but you only gave me one key. Have you another?'

'Of course, but I'll have to come with you.'

'Okay.'

The three of them returned to the house where the agent opened the door. All three entered. The place was soulless and there wasn't a sound. A pervasive smell of curry immediately hit them. A small table in the living room was upturned with papers scattered about on the shabby carpet.

'He could be asleep, I suppose,' said Parveen.

They climbed the stairs hoping to find Mahmood snoring and fast asleep, but there was no sign of him.

'The bed hasn't been slept in. Oh God. Where is he?' exclaimed Parveen. 'What's been happening here? It looks as though there's been a struggle.'

'Don't worry, love, the chances are there's a simple explanation,' said the policeman in an effort to comfort her. 'Wait here while I go and radio in.'

He returned to the police car and just as he reached it, a radio message came through. 'This is Bradford C.I.D.; we are urgently seeking one Parveen Ashkani, an Asian woman in her early thirties. Contact D.I. Turnbull of Bradford murder squad if identified.'

The PC did just that. 'I've got her with me,' he reported to Turnbull.

'Well, bring her in. Don't say anything about why we need to speak to her.'

He returned to the house. 'We need to take you to Bradford headquarters, love; they need to speak to you.'

'Oh God, I knew it. They've killed him.'

She became hysterical and so the policeman and letting agent sat her down. 'You take her straight to Bradford and I'll walk back to my office.'

'Thanks. Okay love, let's go.'

The journey was made with the blue light flashing. Parveen sat in the back, weeping uncontrollably. They were soon at Bradford headquarters where Turnbull was waiting for them.

'Are you Parveen Ashkani?' he asked.

'Yes, what's happened?'

'I'm afraid there's no easy way of telling you this. Your husband's been shot and he's dead.'

———————•◦✕◦•———————

Chapter 5

Parveen Ashkani's Story

Parveen collapsed to the floor. A policewoman went to get some water and some smelling salts kept for such occasions. She eventually revived.

Turnbull assessed her as five feet five inches in height and overweight. She wore traditional Asian clothes, but she was not typical of the Asian women he had come across. She had obviously been born in England and had a westernized air about her.

'I knew this would happen. It's my family,' she said. 'They disapproved of our marriage. They threatened to kill him and now they have. It's my brothers, Nadeem Khan and Wahid Mahmood. They've done it. I've been hiding him from them and they've obviously found out where he lived and killed him. They warned me that if I married him, they would kill him and they have.'

D.I. Turnbull arranged for a policewoman to sit with her whilst she then told her story. D.I. Turnbull decided not to inform her family because of what she was saying about her brothers. He needed her account before they got to her. After that, it was anyone's guess what she would say.

Turnbull, accompanied by the policewoman, took Parveen to an interview room.

'Sit down, lass,' said Turnbull. 'Can we get you a cup of tea?'

'No thanks, I just can't believe what's happened.'

'Well, you tell us in your own time. If you want a break or refreshments, you just tell us. Okay?'

'Thanks.'

Turnbull realized the girl's English was excellent and she

was obviously intelligent. 'Take your time. Let's start by asking how old you are?'

'Twenty-six.'

'Were you born locally?'

'Yes, in Halifax in 1982. I'm one of four children. My parents are Pakistani. They came to the UK many years ago.'

'Tell me about your family.'

'My elder brother, Nadeem Khan, is two years older than me. My younger brother is Wahid Mahmood and he's three years younger than me. My youngest brother is Abdul Mahmood and he's only sixteen. He's in Pakistan.'

'Where do you live now?'

'With my parents in Parkinson Road in Halifax. I've been there for two months.'

'Did you grow up in Halifax?'

'Yes at 22 Bottomley Terrace. I went to local school until I was eight. My mother took me and my brother, Nadeem, to Pakistan. My father's brother lives there. He's called Rashid Khan.'

'Did you and he get on?'

'He was very controlling. That's the custom there. Whenever I went out, I had to be accompanied.'

'How long did you stay there?'

'I was there for several years. My mother came home after eighteen months, leaving me with Nadeem and Uncle Rashid.'

'Did you like it there?'

'No. I wanted to come home and continue my schooling, but my mother said it was important that I learned Pakistani culture from the family.'

'Did you go to school there?'

'Not until I was twelve. I was then allowed to go to school for two or three days a week. The rest of the time I was treated as a skivvy.'

'When did you return?'

'In 1997 when I was fifteen. I'd been there seven years. I could hardly speak a word of English, but I was determined to learn and, as you can tell, through hard work, I can now.'

'What was planned for your future?'

'That I should marry my cousin, Rashid's son.'

'Did you want to?'

'No. I was too young and I wanted to marry someone of my own choice.'

'What happened when you returned to England in 1997?'

'I got a job as a receptionist. In my spare time, I started 'A' level courses at Calderdale College. I am westernized and I believe women have an equal status in society as men.

'The family didn't like it. I'd argue with my brothers and they got angry with me saying that I was out of line and they would hit me. My father encouraged them by saying that I must learn to do as I was told by him and my brothers.'

'Did you go back to Pakistan?'

'Yes, when I was twenty. My father said he'd had enough of my disobedience and that I must go back with Nadeem and Wahid for a holiday to keep up family ties. I finally agreed because I had no choice. Women don't make choices in Pakistani society.'

'So that was when?'

'In 2002. We stayed with Uncle Rashid. The plan was to return in three weeks, but that day came and we were still there. I asked Nadeem when I could go home and he said "When you behave". We had a heated argument and he hit me, telling me not to be disobedient.

'I got very depressed. Wouldn't you? It's awful to be controlled all the time, not being allowed to do as you wish.'

'What was Nadeem doing?'

'He met a girl called Aisha. It was an arranged meeting, but he didn't mind. He liked her. He introduced me to her family. Her brother was Mahmood Asgar who's just been murdered. I can't believe it.'

'What happened when you met Mahmood?'

'Well, we liked each other. We were similar spirits and he was from the same family as Aisha, so I couldn't see the harm. We saw a lot of each other and we fell in love. He is, um I mean was, handsome, dashing and intelligent.'

'What was your family's attitude?'

'They disapproved because my father had promised me to Rashid's son, and he said he wouldn't go back on his word.

'I said Nadeem is going to marry Aisha, so what harm is there in me marrying her brother? They are a very respectable family. What's the problem?

'My father shouted "You will not marry him. You will marry your cousin". My father never adapted to Western culture. He might just as well be still living in Pakistan. He doesn't speak a word of English, nor does my mother, but I was brought up in the UK and appreciate the freedom a woman can enjoy.

'When I said I wouldn't marry my cousin, I was beaten by my brother for being cheeky. They said they would see that our relationship ceased. Despite them, I kept meeting Asgar secretly and in December 2002, he bought me a ticket to return to England. We went to the airport and, at the departure gate, Asgar put an engagement ring on my finger.'

'Did you fly home?'

'Yes and went home to Halifax. I didn't tell my parents that I had secretly got engaged to Asgar.'

'Did you seek anyone's help?'

'Yes, Narinda at the Calderdale Women's Centre. I spoke to her frequently about my problems at home and she was very sympathetic. She is also Asian and she understands the position of Asian women in a Western culture. Can I have a break?'

'Yes, of course. We'll get you some tea. Relax for a while and tell us when you're ready to continue. You're doing very well.'

Turnbull and Jasper left the room, organized some tea for her and went outside for a smoke. They left Parveen and the policewoman alone. Parveen looked numb. Tears ran down her face. She didn't wipe them away but let them drop onto her lap. She stared at the window as if unaware of where she was, as if the whole process was a nightmare.

The tea arrived and she took a sip. She felt alone in a cruel world. She had never been in a police station before, let alone in an interview room with table and chairs bolted to the floor.

She asked, 'Can't my mother come here to be with me?'

'Ask Mr Turnbull,' was the reply. 'But I don't think he wants you talking to those at home until you've finished your statement.'

She just said, 'Oh,' and sat there.

Turnbull and Jasper returned after fifteen minutes. 'Okay?' they asked.

'Yes thanks, but can't my momma come?'

'We'd prefer not just at the moment.'

'Well, we'll continue then. How did you keep in touch with Asgar?'

'I'd telephone Aisha and she would put her brother on the phone. Wahid caught me one day and grabbed the phone from me and broke it.'

'How long did this continue?'

'For about a year, but by then I'd had enough. I'd saved some money from working so, one day, with Narinda's help, I just left and went to Cardiff. I don't know why I chose Cardiff. Maybe it was because there's a big Asian community there.'

'Did you tell anyone where you'd gone?'

'Only Narinda. But I kept my mobile and my brothers would

telephone me and send me texts saying that they'd find me and kill me.'

'Have you kept any of the texts?'

'No.'

'Or the calls?'

'No.'

'Where did you live in Cardiff?'

'With an Asian family. I met them through going to a restaurant when I first arrived and I got talking to a young waiter called Saber Malik. He took pity on me. He also was Pakistani and he asked his mother, who worked in the kitchen, if I could stay with them. She said yes and so I moved in with the family. How lucky was I? We are like that in the community. We help each other.'

'Did you confide in Saber?'

'Yes, I told him I was secretly engaged to Asgar and how I was afraid of my brothers and what they said they'd do if they found me.'

'What was Saber's reaction?'

'He was worried for my safety. He told social services and they sent a policeman to see me. I told him about the threats to kill me and Asgar if he ever came to the UK.'

'So the threats were to him also?'

'Oh yes, all the time.'

'Did the policeman take a statement from you?'

'Yes.'

'Did he ask to see the texts?'

'No.'

'Did you still have some at that stage?'

'Yes.'

Why oh why, thought Turnbull, hadn't the policeman asked to see the texts and then preserved them. As it was, they only had her word that there were threats made.

'What happened next? Here you are, living in Cardiff.'

'Somehow or other, my brothers found out I was in Cardiff. I think I stupidly told my mother and they must have got it out of her.'

'And so what happened?'

'They came to Cardiff, mob-handed, and took me forcibly back to Halifax. I pretended to be contrite and kept my head down.'

'What happened next?'

'Six months later, I returned to Pakistan on the pretext of going to see my cousin whom I'd promised to marry.'

'Did you manage to see Asgar?'

'Yes, we married secretly in Lahore. I ran away with him and lived with him in a village house in Gujarat which his mother and father had found for us.'

Her eyes welled with tears as she remembered. 'How happy we were, and look how it's turned out.'

'Well, I think that's enough for today. We've found a flat for you to stay in overnight, isn't that right officer?'

'Yes,' replied the woman police officer. 'I know it and it's very comfortable. I will go with her.'

'Excellent,' said Turnbull. 'This policewoman will stay with you and look after you, and we'll continue in the morning. I would prefer it if you didn't speak to your family. Okay?'

'Yes, thank you, I need to sleep.'

'I'll bet. We'll see you tomorrow.'

At that point, she left with the policewoman. Turnbull and Jasper went to the nearby pub, the local haunt of staff from HQ, and had a few pints. It was the end of a long working day.

'Well, I think it's going well,' said Jasper.

'I agree,' replied Turnbull. 'But she's not got to the nitty-gritty yet and if she comes up with what we think she'll say about her brothers being responsible, it will be a question of keeping her in line. If she goes back to the family, heaven help her. She'd probably go back on everything.'

They stayed for an hour and then agreed to meet the following morning.

—————•·••·•—————

At 9:00 a.m., in the interview room, they greeted Parveen. She was with the policewoman who looked warm and friendly.

'How are you this morning?' asked Turnbull.

'Okay. I haven't been in touch with my family as you asked, but I rang Asgar's father and he and Asgar's mother are flying over today. I can go and live with them for a while. They are staying with relatives in Hipperholme.'

'Excellent. Now let's return to your account of events. What were your and your husband's plans?'

'I was to return to the UK and he would follow. I'd live with my family. I'd nowhere else to go. I didn't tell them I had married Asgar, but my father's family rang him and said they'd discovered that I'd married him in secret. My family was furious. I denied it, but they didn't believe me. They said this was the end. They would pay to have us both killed. They knew who would do it. It was routine to them. It would cost three or £4,000.'

'Who said that?'

'Nadeem and Wahid.'

Parveen stared at the wall, fidgeting with an ashtray. 'I thought they were bluffing and didn't believe them. None of them had been in trouble for violence. Nadeem was running his restaurant. I never knew what Wahid did, but he seemed normal. How stupid was I?' She looked at Turnbull and shook her head.

'What next?'

'I got a job at a nursing home and started to make arrangements for Asgar to come to England secretly.'

23

'Wasn't that a bit risky?'

'I suppose so, but we were in love and we thought they wouldn't find us.'

'What happened?'

'Well, Asgar got a Pakistani passport in June 2004 and then a visa. Meanwhile, my father didn't believe I'd married Asgar and, despite what the family had told him, was making plans for me to marry my cousin.'

'And then?'

'Well, Asgar flew here in December 2004 and he went to live in Oldham with his uncle and aunt, Bakar Abdul and his wife. I was still with my family in Halifax.'

'Did your husband tell you what he said to Bakar and his wife?'

'Yes, he told them of his fear and said my brothers had threatened him over the telephone when he was in Pakistan. They agreed to him living with them.'

'Did you visit?'

'Oh yes, as often as I could. I'd lie to my family saying I was going to work.'

'Asgar was Aisha's brother. Was she now married to your brother, Nadeem?'

'Yes, but they had broken up over me marrying her brother. Her parents couldn't believe what a family they had let their children marry into. Asgar and Aisha's father is an MP, for God's sake.'

'So Asgar is living in Oldham and you are visiting. How long did this go on for?'

'Oh, weeks. I can't be exact.'

'What happened next?'

'Somehow my brothers found out where he was living. Wahid warned me that he and Nadeem were deadly serious and that the killer had been paid.

'I now believed their threats … that they weren't bluffing but were deadly serious, so I pleaded with Asgar to return to Pakistan for his own safety, but he refused.

'I then found him accommodation in Halifax 'cause I couldn't bear him being so far away. Oh, God, I led him to his death.'

'We all make mistakes, lassie. It's easy to be wise after the event. Can you carry on?' asked Turnbull.

'Yes,' she sobbed. 'I rented the house in Halifax and took Asgar there. I told him to stay inside for his own safety.'

'How did he react to that?'

'He hated it. He said he was giving in and would return to Pakistan in March, in just a few weeks' time. If only they'd left him alone he'd have gone and been out of their hair.'

'What happened next?'

'Well, on Sunday, the sixth of February, I spent the early afternoon with Asgar at his house – that's number eight Grove Road – it's near my family house. We went out in my car to Cannon Mills in Bradford. We just wanted some normal time together.

'Then I dropped him off at his house and promised to take him some food between eight and nine o'clock that night. I told him to lock the door after me.

'I then went swimming and went back to his house with food at eight o'clock. He wasn't there, so I left the food on the doorstep and returned about an hour later. He still wasn't there, so I was really worried and began to panic. I couldn't ring him 'cause I hadn't any credit on my mobile. I thought he must have gone out for a walk; it was a nice evening and he had been complaining about being cooped up in the house. So I went home and went to bed.

'I could hear my father singing to himself "God has listened. What I wanted has happened today. God has helped me". And then I heard Nadeem saying to him "Everything has gone okay". But then I couldn't hear what else he said.'

'And what did you think?'

'I didn't know what to think. I certainly didn't think they'd murdered Asgar. The following morning, yesterday morning, I went back to the house. The food was still there on the doorstep. I panicked. I went to a telephone box and rang his number, but there was no reply.

'Just as I came out of the phone box, a police car was approaching so I flagged it down and told the policeman my worries. He was very kind and went to the house with me. There was no sign of Asgar.

'As we were walking out of the house, the policeman got a message on his mobile or radio, whatever it's called, saying that the Bradford police wanted to speak to a Parveen Ashkani. So he brought me here where I met you and you told me what had happened.

'I can't believe how stupid we've been. I should have taken notice.'

'You've done very well. It can't have been easy,' said Turnbull. 'There's nothing more you can do. We'll take you to your in-laws' house now. They are here now, aren't they?'

'Yes.'

'Come back in the morning and everything you've told us will have been typed up and it will be in the form of a witness statement. You can read it, check it and then sign it as accurate.

'It will say that the statement is true and that you know you will be liable to prosecution if you have wilfully stated in it anything you know to be false, or do not believe to be true. Okay?'

'Yes.'

'We'll see you again tomorrow morning at nine o'clock. We'll collect you and bring you here. Okay?'

'Yes.'

Turnbull and Jasper went back to their office.

'All we can do now is wait and see,' Turnbull sighed.

The statement Parveen made ran to many pages. The following day, she signed the caption to the effect that the statement was true and that she knew she would be liable to prosecution if she stated in it anything which she knew to be false, or did not believe to be true.

Turnbull thanked her for her co-operation. He wondered how she would be treated in the community. She seemed a determined young woman. First impressions were favourable, but if her story was accurate, she would face animosity at home, if not violence.

'Where are you going now?' he asked Parveen. 'I'd prefer you not to go to your home where your brothers are.'

'Don't worry,' she replied. 'I am going to live with my in-laws.'

'Excellent,' said Turnbull.

Turnbull could see real problems in handling her up to trial. She would be in contact with her brothers. He appointed a young woman detective officer to be her liaison officer.

———•◆•———

Chapter 6
The Police Investigation

Detective Jane Rowley was a new member of the murder team. She had been a detective for twelve months, after a period in uniform, and promoted to the homicide team only two weeks earlier. She had, like many other new recruits, been to Bradford University where she got a degree in geography. She was supposedly in the fast lane and this was the first big step out of uniform and into the C.I.D. then, after three months, into the homicide team. She was proud of this promotion.

She was twenty-nine, unmarried, and she liked her independence. Being a police officer wasn't easy. It was hard work and unsocial hours meant she didn't have a boyfriend, although fellow staff seemed to fancy her, but she didn't want a relationship with a policeman. If that happened, their whole life would revolve around work and she didn't want that.

She remembered one night, when she was with South Yorkshire Police, getting drunk at a party and sleeping with a detective sergeant. The following morning, there were cat calls and whistles in the squad room. She resolved never again and applied for a transfer to Bradford. Good move.

Early the following day, Turnbull despatched her to find Narinda, the counsellor from Calderdale who had befriended Parveen, to see if she would corroborate Parveen's account.

'Treat her with kid gloves. She may be very defensive of her client and not willing to say anything,' Turnbull had said.

The Calderdale Women's Centre was a dreary, dilapidated building on Harrison Road in Halifax. It had been a terrace house, but converted into offices. At the front was an untended garden with a profusion of tall weeds and discarded Kentucky

Fried Chicken cartons.

She was let in by someone who she assumed was a volunteer. Jane said who she was and that she wanted to speak to Narinda.

'Narinda is a pseudonym. She is a professional counsellor. What's it about?'

'I'd prefer to speak to Narinda about it if you don't mind,' replied Jane.

'Hold on, I'll see if she's in. She usually is at this time. Can I get you a coffee?'

'Yes please, white no sugar.'

'Please sit down and I'll get you a coffee and see if Narinda is in.'

The lady disappeared and Jane sat in the room. which was a bit like a doctors' waiting room. Old, well-thumbed magazines littered the table and the wallpaper was peeling off the walls. *This place is run on a shoestring,* she thought.

The volunteer returned about five minutes later with an Asian lady in her fifties with white hair swept back into a bun. She wore a white polo-necked sweater, brown trousers with a belt and brown shoes. *Very neat,* thought Jane.

'Can I help you?' she asked.

'I hope so,' replied Jane. 'Do you go by the name Narinda?'

'Yes I do,' she said.

'I'm Detective Jane Rowley from the Bradford homicide squad. We're conducting a murder investigation. A man called Mahmood Asgar has been murdered. He was married to Parveen Ashkani. Can you tell me if you spoke to her at any time?'

'Yes.'

'Can you tell me what Parveen Ashkani said to you concerning her brothers?'

'Well, it's not that easy, I'm afraid. What is said to us is in confidence and we can't just allow what is said to us to be put into the public domain.'

'Well, I assure you that the homicide squad is not the public domain. The girl's husband has been murdered and we have strong reason to believe that her brothers may be behind it. Anything she said about her brothers is, therefore, very material to our enquiries.

'Your status is not equivalent to a lawyer's but, if you wish, I can get a judge's order that you disclose this information. That will take a little time and will delay our investigations.'

'Well, I see that,' said Narinda. 'May I ask – did Parveen tell you about coming to me for help?'

'Yes, she did and I'm sure she would have no objections to your telling us what she said to you.'

'Very well, I'll get my notes.'

Narinda disappeared and then returned.

'This is confidential so you'd better come to an interview room.'

Jane followed her along a narrow passage and into a small room with a table, two chairs and a window looking out on to Harrison Road and what passed for a garden.

'Here's the report I made at the time. Do you want me to read it out?'

'Yes please.'

'It reads, "Parveen is suffering violence at home. Things are not too bad at the moment but, in the past, her brothers – especially the eldest – have physically assaulted her. Problems are arising because Parveen doesn't want to go to Pakistan. When everything has calmed down, everyone is apologetic and it seems as though nothing has happened.". Two weeks later, she reported to me that her brothers were watching her every move. She felt very isolated so I arranged for her to go to Cardiff. She telephoned me from there saying that her brothers had been threatening to kill her.

'I never heard from her after that. I assumed that things had settled down. I didn't report it. We hear so much.'

'How did she seem?' asked Jane.

'Very upset.'

'And you thought she was genuine?'

'Oh yes. We do get false complaints, but this didn't strike me as being false.'

'Thanks,' said Jane 'we'll be in touch again.' She noted no threats to kill her husband.

Back at headquarters, she reported to Turnbull.

'Well, sir, she certainly spoke to Narinda and reported her fear of her brothers. But Narinda didn't mention any bruises and such like.'

'Hmm,' said Turnbull. 'We will have to be aware that Parveen herself could be creating a background to the killing which portrays her as the victim so as to enable her to kill him. She could be extremely devious and leading us up the garden path. But I think that very unlikely. She would have killed within the house, not taken him up to the moors. And her demeanour, when she came here, seemed to be totally genuine.'

'I agree,' said Jane. 'I think that, so far, what she has said is a true account, but whether she sticks to it is the question.'

'I agree, Jane. Now can you go to Cardiff? See if the family she stayed with have anything to say. Also, find the PC she spoke to.'

'Certainly,' said Jane.

The following day, she drove to Cardiff. It was a long journey in the rain. With the help of her Garmin, she found the address Parveen had given them on the outskirts of Cardiff. Judging by the number of Indian restaurants, it was a predominantly immigrant area. She thought of Shirley Bassey growing up here.

She knocked on the door and a young Asian boy answered.

'Are you Saber Malik?' she asked him.

'Yes please.'

'I'm Detective Jane Rowley from the Bradford Homicide Unit. May I come in?'

'Of course,' said Saber. 'But I'm going to work soon. I'm a waiter at our family restaurant.'

'This shouldn't take too long,' said Jane.

'I suppose it's about Parveen?' Saber asked.

'Yes,' said Jane. 'You guessed right. How old are you?'

'Sixteen. I left school last year. I was born here so I can speak English, but I go to evening classes to improve. I want to own my own restaurant in time, but I'm learning the ropes and cooking stuff with my mum and dad's help.'

'Good for you,' said Jane. 'Can you tell me how you met Parveen and what happened after you'd met?'

'Yes, of course. She came into the restaurant and I took pity on her,' he said. 'Because she said she had suitcases with her and nowhere to live. I agreed, after asking my mother, that she could come and live at our house. She stayed for two months. She told me there were family problems. Her brothers wouldn't let her out of the house. They beat her up. She said she didn't want to see her brothers.

'She had married some guy in Pakistan and the brothers didn't like it. She was scared that if the brothers caught her, they would kill her. She was scared her brothers would find her. Then they did and they took her away. There were about forty of them. They brought lots of cars. I ran to the toilet and rang the police, but she had gone by the time they arrived.'

'Thanks,' said Jane. 'You did well to look after her. Are you willing to make a statement about what you've just told me?'

'Of course, if it will help. What's happened?'

'I'm afraid her husband has been murdered and we're

investigating the background to it. You've been a great help. Thank you, Saber.'

'Send her my love, please.'

'Of course.'

Next, she went to find the PC who had visited Parveen in Cardiff. She went to Cardiff Central Police Station and explained her problem to the sergeant on duty at the desk. He checked his computer and said, 'Yes, she was visited by a community PC called Ashwood.'

'May I see him, please?'

'He's not here, but he's due back in a few minutes. Please sit and wait in my office. Can I get you a coffee?'

'Dying for one,' said Jane.

Ten minutes later, a community PC about forty years old came in. Jane's first impression was that he wasn't the sharpest knife in the drawer.

He introduced himself to Jane.

'What can you tell me?'

'Well,' he said. 'I went to see her at the request of a woman called Narinda at the Calderdale Women's Centre in Halifax. Parveen had received a text message from her brothers threatening to kill her.'

'What did you do?' asked Jane.

'I reported it,' he said.

'And nothing more?' asked Jane. 'You never asked to see the texts?'

'No,' he replied.

How stupid, she thought.

'Well, what happened?'

'I don't know. I did my job and reported it. What happened after that was not up to me.'

Jane returned to the sergeant. 'Did this enquiry just die then?' she asked.

'It seems so. We get a lot of domestics here and we're undermanned.'

'Thanks,' said Jane, and, under her breath, 'for nothing.'

Chapter 7

Case Conference

D.I. James Turnbull met with his team, as arranged, at the police headquarters in Bradford. The meeting was presided over by Detective Superintendent Bob Illingworth, a long time Bradford copper who had risen through the ranks and was now nearing retirement. He knew James Turnbull well and had put him in charge of the Bradford Homicide Crime Unit some years before. They were friends outside work and each had an allotment in Idle, Bradford. Both had been involved with the Bradford riots.

Since then, there had been a spate of Asian killings and gang warfare that he could have well done without, but it wouldn't be long before he retired and could concentrate on his allotment. Meanwhile, he would lead this investigation.

Present were D.I. James Turnbull, D.S. Dave Jasper, Detective Jon Crawford, a stenographer and Bob Illingworth who opened the proceedings.

'Tell us what you've got, Jim.'

'Well, sir, on the face of it we have quite a lot, but this may prove to be illusory. The dead man we now know is Mahmood Asgar. For shortness, I will call him Asgar. He is, or should I say was, a thirty-two-year-old Pakistani who was married to Parveen Ashkani. She was born in Halifax of Pakistani parents.

'In summary, he married Parveen in Pakistan against her family's wishes. Her father and her brothers, Nadeem Khan and Wahid Mahmood, were against it even though Nadeem is, or should we say was, married to Asgar's sister.

'The names are complicated, as is the story but, in short, according to Parveen who has made a long witness statement, quite willingly and without prevarication, the two brothers and the father threatened that they would have the pair of them killed for marrying against the family's wishes. Mother sat on the fence.

'They said to Parveen that they would pay for the killing, so we are probably looking for paid assassins. The talk was of paying three or £4,000 so, if that happened, they are pretty small fry and, with leads, we should find them. So, although I thought it might be a drug-war killing or purely racialist, I'm now satisfied it was an "honour killing".

'What leads have you got?' asked Illingworth.

'So far, we've no leads other than there were three, probably white, men at the scene in a vehicle that Jon Crawford, here present, who happened to be passing the scene shortly after the killing, thought was a Peugeot 405 old model or a Rover 414.

'Parveen doesn't know who her brothers hired and they could be from anywhere. We've put the usual feelers out to informants but, so far, nothing. What she says rings true. We tried to put her in a safe house but she refused. She's gone to live with her in-laws, but for how long we don't know. If she goes back to her family then they are the very people she says were responsible for the death.'

'Is she in danger?'

'No, I don't think so. She is family after all. But I've no doubt they'll get at her to change her statement.'

'The chances are she'll go back on what she has told us. Whether we get her witness statement in evidence at their trial, if it gets that far, will depend upon whether the trial judge allows her to be treated as a hostile witness and allows her witness statement to be admitted in evidence. If she's clever and does not appear hostile to the prosecution, she may avoid that happening. As you probably know, if the judge decides that she is not wanting to tell the truth, he may allow prosecution counsel to cross-examine her upon her witness statement.

'Otherwise, at present, we've no leads. Nothing, so far, has materialised in forensic evidence from the scene and we've no way of keeping Parveen sweet.'

'So we have Parveen's statement implicating her brothers but nothing else,' said Illingworth.

'That's right,' said Turnbull.

'Thanks,' said Illingworth. 'Anyone anything to add?'

'Can I play devil's advocate for a moment?' asked Jasper. 'We only have her word for it that her brothers beat her. Perhaps witnesses will emerge who saw her with injuries, but somehow I doubt it.

'What if she decided the marriage wasn't working and she wanted rid of him? She had, after all, lived with him for several weeks in Pakistan.

'What if she sets up a scenario in advance by telling Narinda and the guy in Cardiff that her brothers beat her and then she arranges for him to be brought to the UK with the idea of having him killed here? She is a bright woman who I suspect we will see is well capable of such a scheme.

'Thereby, she puts blame on her brothers and avoids herself being identified as a possible killer.'

'Well,' said Turnbull. 'I suppose it's possible. I'd already thought of that and that's all the more reason to look for corroboration of her story.'

'And what of the younger brother?' asked Jasper. 'He has apparently hopped it to Pakistan. He was only sixteen, but what a coincidence that he hops it just as his brother-in-law is murdered. The elder brothers aren't the only possible culprits.'

Dave Jasper liked to put his oar in from time to time. He crossed his legs and, in his Austin Reed suit, preened himself whilst the others took in what he had said.

'It's true. It's difficult for us to get under the skin of these

Asian families,' said Illingworth.

There was a silence.

'Maybe also these brothers have blabbed locally,' said Dave Jasper. 'We can try that route.'

'The problem,' said Turnbull. 'Is that they will probably only have talked to Asians and you know what it's like getting some to talk to the police. It's like drawing teeth and even then, from past experience, there's a question mark over reliability. That's realistic, not racist.'

'Okay,' said Illingworth. 'Let's meet at the same time tomorrow. Something may have come up by then. In the meantime, do what you can. You know there were three killers, probably white, probably in a Peugeot 405 or a Rover 414. Follow those leads. Meeting closed.'

James Turnbull went back to his office with Dave Jasper. He called Jon Crawford and the rest of the team into his office. 'Jon, go look at images of cars to check your opinion as to the type.'

'Will do,' said Jon.

'The rest of you concentrate on the two brothers and ascertain whether they were known to the police. Also, recover as many CCTV recordings as possible, within a two mile radius of the deceased's home, looking for a Peugeot 405 or a Rover 414, old model going to or from 8 Grove Road.'

James thought things were moving on, but still had no clue as to who the assassins were.

He resisted smoking a cigarette because the smoke offended Dave.

Chapter 8

Further Investigations

D.I. Turnbull and D.S. Jasper next went to see Nadeem Khan – they both considered him to be the most likely principal behind the murder as, if Parveen was accurate, he was the one who had threatened to kill her husband and who had money as he was a successful businessman.

Nadeem was the proprietor of a popular Asian restaurant in Halifax. They thought it best to tackle him there, rather than at his home. When they arrived, at 6:00 p.m., a Porsche 911 with a personalized number plate was parked outside. This caused Turnbull to think that here was a man who could afford to pay killers. How did he afford such a car? As a drug peddler?

The restaurant was typical of hundreds in West Yorkshire but it was well-kept, with the usual menu in the window. The site was good, just off Harrison Road in the town centre. The pervasive smell of curry met them.

They were early so banged on the door. Eventually it was answered by a cook.

'Can we see Nadeem Khan? We're from the police.'

'I suppose so. I'll take you to his office. It's in the back. He's always early.'

Nadeem was in good shape, physically, with designer stubble. He was wearing an open-neck shirt, a two-piece single-breasted suit and a gold bracelet on his wrist.

With his car, thought Turnbull, *he looks the young Asian about town.*

'We're investigating the murder of Mahmood Asgar last Sunday night at about eight o'clock. Do you know anything about it?' asked D.I. Turnbull.

'No, nothing,' he said.

'Where were you at 8:00 p.m. last Sunday?' asked Turnbull.

'Here,' replied Nadeem. 'Who's this man Asgar?'

'He's your brother-in-law,' replied Turnbull.

'No,' said Nadeem. 'I only have one sister and she's not married.'

'Yes she is,' replied Turnbull. 'She married Asgar in Pakistan. You know that and you've been out to kill him ever since.'

'I know nothing of any Asgar,' said Nadeem. 'I'm a businessman. I've no knowledge of what you say. I was here at 8:00 p.m. on Sunday. My staff will verify that.'

'Where is your brother, Wahid?' asked Turnbull.

'You should know,' said Nadeem. 'He's in prison, so he couldn't have done it either.'

Turnbull was taken aback by this information, but told him they would see him again and left.

Wahid being in prison was a turn up for the books. *Maybe he orchestrated the murder from prison,* thought Turnbull. He remembered the film *The Italian Job* with Noel Coward and smiled. It was a great film also starring Michael Caine. The new version wasn't nearly so good.

He wondered why Parveen had neglected to tell them that Wahid was in prison. He felt stupid for not having checked antecedents earlier.

'What do you think?' he asked Jasper in the car.

'Well, of the two, he was in circulation, but if his brother is a villain, he may have the contacts.'

Back at the police station, Turnbull got on his computer and made enquiries about Wahid. It was true; he was in prison serving three and a half years for supplying Class A controlled drugs.

At least he'll be easy to find and also he would have plenty of money to pay assassins, thought Turnbull. *Which of the two brothers was the leader?*

Chapter 9
The Car

On Wednesday, the 9th February, 2005, PC Allan Dawson and his partner, Dan Gibson, were on mobile patrol in Sheffield. They drove near Tinsley Golf Club and saw a Rover car parked on a rough track leading to a bridle path.

'What do you think that's doing parked there?'

'Maybe someone from the golf club left it there.'

'Funny place to leave it.'

'Nowt so queer as folk. We'll keep tabs on it.'

Two hours later they were back on the same spot.

'I don't believe it. It's been on fire.' The car was burnt out, a smouldering wreck with smoke pouring from the sides of the bonnet.

The two constables went to the car.

'Could this be the car Halifax is looking for? We'd better radio in its details. We probably should have done it when we first saw it. Shit. Anyway let's do it.'

'Rover 414, reg number M835 GVU. Found burnt out near to Tinsley Golf Club. Instructions please. Over.'

'Preserve at all costs. Over.'

'Will do. Over.'

Turnbull and Jasper, who were at headquarters, immediately received the news and gave the instructions.

Turnbull said, 'Now we are getting somewhere.'

Then, to his opposite number in Sheffield, he said, 'Keep the car, we're coming over.'

Jasper contacted DVLA on the direct line which the police have. 'Can you tell me the registered keeper of a Rover M835 GVU?'

He was told to hold on and moments later the girl came back on the line. 'It's registered to Joe Ogden, 46 Weeton Terrace, Sheffield SH17 0AB.'

'Many thanks.'

'Things are looking up,' said Dave. 'If we get an angle on the assassins, they may finger the family.'

'I agree,' replied Turnbull.

Turnbull and Jasper set off for Sheffield. As they got to the M1 going south, they encountered roadworks and the reduction of the speed limit to fifty miles per hour.

'God, when are these roadworks going to finish? It seems it's been like this forever.'

It was downcast, raining and slow.

They found the owner's address via SatNav.

They rang the doorbell.

A man in his fifties answered the door. He was wearing overalls.

'You just caught me,' he said. 'I was just going out on my window cleaning round. What d'ya want?'

'We're police officers from the Bradford Homicide Unit. We're making enquiries about a Rover car M835 GVU. You are shown as the registered keeper. Are you Joe Ogden?'

'Yes, but I'm no longer the registered keeper. I sold the car last Friday.'

'Well, the car has been found burnt out on a remote track near Tinsley Golf Club.'

'Good God,' said Ogden. 'Come in.'

The two officers followed Ogden into his house. They were invited to sit in the living room and did so.

'Tell us about it,' said Turnbull.

'Well, I advertised it in the *Free Ads Magazine.* A man tele-phoned me about four o'clock last Friday saying that he wanted to see the car as soon as possible. He came about an hour later, went for a short drive with me in it and then said he'd have it. He didn't haggle about the price and paid me £310 in cash, which was £10 more than I'd asked for it. Then he drove it away – end of story.'

'Did he give a name?'

'No, I just gave him the log book to send his details off to DVLA.'

'Would you be able to recognize him?'

'No, I don't think so.'

'So, you no longer had the car last Sunday?' asked Turnbull.

'Definitely not,' replied Ogden.

'Well, you've been very helpful. Thank you, Mr Ogden. We'll be in touch,' said Turnbull. 'I'll send a detective to get your statement.'

Mr Ogden gave them his telephone number and promised to give a statement the following day.

Now Turnbull and Jasper knew they may have found the car used in the murder.

There seemed little point in having Forensics examine the car as it was now a burnt out wreck and the purpose of setting it on fire was to destroy any forensic evidence which might be found.

They stopped for a pint at The Greyhound at Tong Village, outside Bradford.

'I like this pub,' said Jasper. 'Better than those spit and sawdust pubs you choose in Bradford.'

'You snob,' said Turnbull. 'This is a puff's parlour, not a pub.'

Meanwhile, the car was recovered and taken to the Bradford headquarters, where there were complaints about it taking up precious space. No police garage was ever big enough.

How to get the man's identity? was Turnbull's thought as he sank his pint.

Chapter 10

Investigation Continued

D.I. Turnbull was at his desk the following day, after the 8:00 a.m. meeting, when his phone rang. It was the SOCO, Bill Thornton, in charge of the forensic work.

'James, we've had a huge breakthrough. We found a cigarette butt at the murder scene. We recovered it to see if the smoker had left his DNA on it. It's just come back from analysis and we've definitely got some. You should look for a match on your database. I suppose it could've been dropped by someone unconnected with the murder, but it's unlikely in such a remote spot.'

'Fantastic,' said Turnbull. 'The miracles of science. Well done. I'll get back to you.'

D.I. Turnbull rang his sergeant, who was out of the office, to tell him the news and frantic searches for a comparison began when the DNA details had been emailed through. *Thank God for DNA,* thought Turnbull, what *did we do when we didn't have it?*

He knew that everyone, except identical twins, has a unique DNA; that DNA is a complex chemical found in cells throughout the human body and that if someone deposits saliva on a cigarette end, the saliva can be analyzed to determine the DNA profile of that person. It is then possible to see if that person's DNA matches with anyone on their database. It did – it matched a man called Sam Leonard who, at the time of his last conviction, lived in Sheffield.

Could this man be one of the three seen by Jon Crawford? Turnbull wondered. This fits with the car being found in Sheffield.

Sam Leonard had a record, but not much of one. He had convictions for assault and shop burglary. Fortunately, at the time of his arrest for those offences some years earlier, a sample of his blood had been taken, his DNA determined and it had since been stored on the police database.

D.I. Turnbull knew that the chances of anyone else, with the same DNA, smoking that cigarette at the scene of the murder were one in a million. He now probably had a murderer, or at least someone who had been at the scene of the murder.

Chapter 11
Sam Leonard

D.I. Turnbull decided to approach Sam Leonard early, so as to catch him unawares. He and Dave Jasper traced him through social security records to an address in Sheffield. They drove down the M1 which, at that hour, was quiet.

Leonard lived in a flat in a high-rise block. The lift to the seventh floor, where he lived, didn't work. The ground floor smelt of urine and the walls were covered with graffiti. They toiled their way up to the seventh floor, taking a breather after four floors.

'You need to improve your fitness, Dave,' commented Turnbull.

'I know, it's too much beer,' he replied.

At approximately 6:00 a.m. they knocked on Leonard's door and a bleary-eyed man answered. 'Yes?' he said. 'What do you want at this hour? I was working late last night.'

The man was in his forties and was wearing jeans, a string vest and bedroom slippers. He was overweight, which made Turnbull wonder how he managed to climb the stairs to the seventh floor. He was unshaven and he had tattoos over what could be seen of his body, except his face.

'We are from the Bradford Homicide Crime Unit. Detective Inspector Turnbull and Detective Sergeant Jasper. Are you Sam Leonard?'

'Yes, what of it?'

'Can we come in?'

'I suppose so,' said Leonard as he led them into an untidy sitting room. The flat smelt of dirty nappies. He didn't seem nervous, which was not a good sign.

'We're here about a murder last Sunday night, on the moors outside Bradford, at about eight o'clock. We know you were involved, Sam,' said Turnbull.

'What are you talking about?' Leonard replied.

'An Asian man called Mahmood Asgar was shot in the back at close range on the moors between Bradford and Halifax. He's dead. You and two others did it.'

'No way,' said Sam as he lit a cigarette.

'We have strong evidence that you were at the scene of this murder. We're arresting you on suspicion of the murder of Mahmood Asgar. Get dressed.'

Leonard dressed and was then taken to Bradford police station in the car, in which he promptly fell asleep.

There had been no conversation en route. Turnbull didn't want any suggestions of "verballing", i.e. an allegation of attributing to him a confession which he said he never made.

On arrival, Leonard was put in an interview room. He immediately said, 'I want my solicitor.'

'Just answer this,' said Turnbull. 'Have you ever been on the moor road between Bradford and Halifax?'

'No way,' replied Leonard.

'Fair enough,' said Turnbull. 'I should tell you that your DNA has been recovered from the scene of a murder. You were there. You know there is no way out of DNA, so think on.'

Turnbull and Jasper then got a search warrant from the local Magistrates' Court and returned to Sam Leonard's flat in Sheffield to carry out a thorough search, leaving Leonard in custody in the cells.

Once again, they climbed the stairs to the seventh floor. A woman answered the door. 'Are you Mrs Leonard?' Turnbull asked.

'Yes,' she replied.

They introduced themselves.

'What's happened?' she asked.

'We've arrested Sam for murder.'

'Oh, my God.'

'We've got a search warrant to search this flat and take away anything which we believe may connect Sam with the murder. Can you give us his mobile phone please?'

'Yes, it's here somewhere.' She searched the room and found it on the dresser. 'Sam'll want it back,' she said as she handed the phone to Turnbull.

Mrs Leonard was a short woman, in her forties, and somewhat overweight. She had dyed blonde hair and was wearing her dressing gown and slippers. She sat whilst the flat was searched. Nothing of interest was found.

'I'm sorry for the intrusion, love. Sam will be able to ring you shortly,' said Jasper as they made their way out of the flat.

As they set off back in the car, Turnbull said to Jasper. 'We must target telephone numbers. If the brothers' numbers were in touch with Sam Leonard's number then that will be crucial evidence of a link between them. Set on a young D.C. to do the searches. Jane Rowley would be a good bet.'

'Consider it done,' said Jasper.

Leonard's solicitor, Mr. Hyams of Hyams and Reed Solicitors of Leeds, was waiting for them at Bradford C.I.D. headquarters.

'Thanks for coming and waiting, Mr Hyams,' said Turnbull. 'Your client's DNA has been recovered from a cigarette butt found at the scene of a murder. 'Go and see him and we'll interview him again in an hour.'

An hour later, Turnbull and Jasper saw Leonard again in the presence of Mr Hyams and interviewed him under caution.

'Where were you last Sunday night at eight o'clock?'

'Working at the Rose and Crown in Sheffield. I'm a doorman there. I was there with my mate, Omar Fazal.' Turnbull wondered if Fazal could be the second or third man.

'Who do you work for?' asked Turnbull.

'Doormen Incorporated. They supply door staff for pubs.'

'So you were working at the Rose and Crown on Sunday night at eight o'clock?'

'Yes,' said Leonard.

'That's all we're going to ask you for now. Do you mind waiting?'

'No, I'll wait,' said Mr Hyams.

'We'll see you again shortly,' said Turnbull.

D.I. Turnbull went to his office with Jasper and telephoned Doormen Incorporated. An Asian woman answered, 'Doorman Incorporated.'

Turnbull said, 'I'm sorry to trouble you, love. I am a police officer making enquiries about your staffing rota for last Sunday night.'

'I'll put you on to Mr Aziz,' she replied. 'Hold on.' Turnbull waited a few minutes.

'Aziz here.'

Turnbull said, 'I'm a police officer from Bradford Central. Can you tell me if Sam Leonard worked for you last Sunday night?'

'Hold on, Sir,' said Aziz. 'I'll check.'

He came back after a couple of minutes. 'Yes, he's down here as working with Omar Fazal at the Rose and Crown in Sheffield from 8:00 p.m. 'til midnight. Does that help?'

'Yes, thanks, can we come and see you to look at your records?'

'Yes, but they're just jottings in my diary. The labour we use is casual.'

'Do you pay cash or by cheque?' asked Turnbull.

'Cash, minimum wage per hour.'

'Can we come tomorrow?'

'Yes, you're welcome.'

Turnbull and Jasper returned to the interview room.

'We have to make further enquiries. Meanwhile, you'll be held in custody. We will interview you again tomorrow. Thank you, Mr Hyams, we'll contact you and arrange a further interview.'

They returned to their office.

'What do you think?' asked Jasper.

'I don't know. Aziz sounded a bit shifty. Maybe they set up the alibi in advance,' said Turnbull. 'We'll follow it up tomorrow.'

Chapter 12
Case Conference

At 8:00 a.m. the following morning, a case conference was held at Bradford police headquarters in what was optimistically called "The Board Room". Coffee and biscuits had been kindly set out. Detective Superintendent Illingworth was in the chair. To his right sat James Turnbull. Also present were Detective Sergeant Jasper, Detective Constable Crawford and Detective Jane Rowley.

'You lead off, James,' said the superintendent to Turnbull.

'Thank you,' said Turnbull. 'So far we have five suspects. The organizers, Nadeem Khan and Wahid Mahmood, neither of whom was present at the scene of the murder but who we suspect paid three assassins. The fee suggested, according to Parveen, was three thousand or thereabouts.

'We have strong evidence against Leonard – namely, his cigarette tab at the scene. He has denied ever going there so he's not saying he dropped a butt there on a different occasion. However, his employer says he was working that night. We have some evidence against Fazal, whom it seems was with Leonard that night; and some evidence against a man who bought the car which was probably used in the murder and which was burnt out after the murder, days after it was purchased. So far, we have no ID of him.

'The only evidence we have against Nadeem Khan is his sister's account of threats to kill. The same with Wahid Mahmood who, at the time of the killing, was serving a sentence of three and a half years' imprisonment. Parveen will possibly go back to live with the family, so the chances are she will retract her statement – which is the only evidence we have, thus far, implicating the two brothers, although it's obvious the killers had no motive except money. The only motive thus far revealed is the brothers' opposition to the marriage of Parveen and Asgar.

'However, as Dave here has pointed out, we can't rule out Parveen having recruited the killers. We only have her word against her brothers and ample reason for blaming them.

'We need evidence of contact between these people. We need more evidence of animosity by the brothers towards Asgar. We need evidence which indicates that they had a common purpose, namely to kill Mahmood Asgar. We need evidence of who the car buyer was.'

Illingworth suggested, 'Why not go to the Rose and Crown, get the CCTV of the pub and see if it shows them on the night of the murder?'

'That is planned,' replied Turnbull. 'Apparently Wahid's in prison serving three and a half years for supplying Class A drugs. We need to see if the facts of that offence demonstrate a propensity to use violence. It's unlikely, but violence and drugs are often connected. If his record involved violence, it would help.'

Illingworth said, 'As Wahid's in prison, we need to see who he's shared cells with and what he said to his cellmates. Prisoners tend to blab to each other. Wahid may have bragged about the killing. We need to find out where Nadeem and Wahid got the money to pay the assassins. Nadeem seems wealthy so he's probably the source. The killers may also have bragged to partners or whatever.'

'Jane,' Turnbull said to DC Rowley. 'Parveen has told us that there were threats over the phone to Asgar at his home in Halifax, so see which phones have rung that home number.'

Illingworth said, 'James, can you go to a Judge to get an order confiscating the phones belonging to these two? See how active Leonard's and Fazal's phones were at the time of the murder.'

'We already have some of those enquiries in place,' said Turnbull. 'But thanks for your input.'

Illingworth said, 'We need to know who bought the car. Dave, go and see Joe Ogden again and get his phone records. They'll show incoming calls, so check them with him. He should be able to eliminate non-suspicious calls. Then check what's left. With a bit of luck, the buyer used his own phone.

'Will do,' said Dave.

'Excellent,' said Illingworth. 'The investigation seems to be going well.'

———◆◆◆◆◆———

Chapter 13
Joe Ogden

Dave Jasper rang Joe Ogden and was relieved to find him in. *There's a stroke of luck,* he thought.

'Mr Ogden, I need to come to see you about the telephone call from the man who bought your car. Have you got a phone record of your incoming calls?'

'No, but I can get one. It must be due any minute.'

'Will you ring your service provider and ask them to email you with the details? Tell them it's a police enquiry and it's urgent.'

'Will do. My wife has a computer, so it can come through on that.'

'Good. Then check the numbers and see if you can identify the number which details the call from the man interested in buying your car. By the time I get there, hopefully you'll have identified the number. I'll be with you in about an hour.'

'Okay, see you.'

Dave arrived at Joe Ogden's house about an hour and a half later.

'Sorry about the delay. The sooner the M1 is improved, the better.'

'Come in. Want a coffee?' asked Ogden.

'Ta.'

'Well, I've done quite well. O2 sent me the details and I think I've identified the call.'

'Good. Show me.'

Ogden then produced his mobile phone statement on which he'd written, against each incoming call, the names of all the callers but one. The number was 07883-922-100.

'So that's the only number you don't recognise?' asked Jasper.

'Yes.'

'Okay, so now can you get O2 on the phone for me?'

'Sure thing,' said Ogden as he scrolled through his contact list and rang O2. When it started to ring, he handed the phone to Jasper.

'This is Detective Sergeant Dave Jasper of Bradford homicide squad. I am with Mr Joe Ogden who has just spoken to your company and you have kindly emailed him the details of his incoming calls. I am particularly interested in one of the calls from the number 07883-922-100. Can you tell me the identity of the subscriber whose number that is?'

'Well, I don't know. I'll ask my supervisor.'

'Surely Mr Ogden is entitled to know who rang him.'

'Wait a moment.'

She returned to the phone. 'I've spoken to my supervisor and he says I can give the details to Mr Ogden himself and no one else.'

'Well, Mr Ogden is here. He'll speak to you. I'll put him on.'

'Hello, Mr Ogden,' she said. 'I'll have to go through a few security questions first.'

Once the formalities were completed, full name, date of birth, postcode, she gave him the information. Ogden wrote down the subscriber's name and thanked the girl from O2.

'Well?' enquired Jasper.

'It's a man called Jack Rastrick.'

Chapter 14

The Post Mortem – Forensics

In the meantime, a detailed post mortem was carried out on the body of Asgar by Professor John Talbot. He met Turnbull in his office at the University of Leeds. They knew each other of old and had worked together on numerous homicides in the past. Talbot had opened the Forensic Pathology Unit at Leeds and had a worldwide reputation.

'Good to see you, John, long time no see,' said Turnbull.

'True,' replied Talbot. 'We're all too busy.'

'What have you got?' asked Turnbull.

Talbot said, 'Asgar had been shot three times, once in the leg and twice, at close range, in the back. I think he was kneeling when he was shot at close range from behind. One bullet hit his ribcage and lodged in his neck. The other went straight through his heart and exited, causing massive bleeding and death.

'The third bullet, I surmised from its shape, had ricocheted, possibly off a wall, and entered his leg. What killed him was the bullet through his heart. At least he would have died almost instantly.'

'How far behind him do you reckon the gunman would have stood?' asked Turnbull.

Professor Talbot demonstrated as he replied, 'A matter of feet and he would have been pointing at the deceased as he knelt down in front of him or below him.'

'Thanks, John.'

'Do you want to see the body? You won't learn much. It's been dissected and put back together again for the funeral.'

'No need,' said Turnbull. 'You've told me all I need to know.'

'This is my third autopsy today,' said Talbot. 'Don't rush back.'

———◆◆◆◆———

Meanwhile, at the Home Office Laboratory in Wetherby, Bill Thornton examined the items his team had recovered from the scene and the body.

The material he found suggested at least three rounds of ammunition had been fired, possibly four. He had found a bullet jacket very close to a wall and it was there he had also found a spent round of ammunition.

From experience and examination of the bullet and cartridge case, he knew that the gun which had been fired was a Russian Baikal-branded starter-pistol which had been adapted to fire conventional 9mm ammunition. It would be an automatic pistol. Recently, these pistols had been prevalent in shootings all over the country.

To be sure, he sent the cartridge to the Specialist Forensic Department at the laboratory and they confirmed his opinion.

He reduced his findings to writing and sent them off to James Turnbull. The firearms expert did likewise.

———◆◆◆◆———

Chapter 15
Sam Leonard

Later that morning, D.I. Turnbull went to Bradford Crown Court where, in chambers, he obtained an order confiscating the mobile phones of all five suspects from the Recorder of Bradford, Bradford's most senior judge. He already had two phones but a belt-and-braces approach was necessary if there were, as was likely, more phones attributable to suspects Leonard, Fazal, Rastrick, Nadeem, Wahid and, to be safe, Parveen Ashkani. He explained to the judge in chambers why he wanted the order and it was granted immediately.

Turnbull then returned to Bradford police headquarters and re-interviewed Sam Leonard again in the presence of his solicitor.

'Sorry to drag you back,' he said to Hyams, 'but as you'd expect, there are developments.'

Before anything was said, Leonard piped up. 'I made a mistake when I last spoke to you because I'm not sure whether I was at work last Sunday night. I might have been confused with the week before. I had the night off work because I didn't feel well. I spent the evening at home with the wife.'

'You weren't out with Omar Fazal then?' enquired Turnbull.

Leonard shook his head. 'No, I got confused. I was at home all evening.'

'Doing what?'

'Watching TV.'

'What programme?'

'Some documentary about the war.'

'Okay, we'll see you again,' said Turnbull. Turnbull knew he would have to charge Leonard very soon or release him.

Chapter 16
The CCTV Recording

Having been told by Turnbull of Leonard's version of events – namely, that he was not working at the Rose and Crown on the Sunday night in question – Crawford went to see whether he had been there or not.

The pub was a typical tied house with a mock Tudor exterior and fruit machines inside. A jukebox was blaring out pop music, which Crawford couldn't stand.

He found the manageress, June Hellawell.

'Hello, love,' he said. 'We're investigating a murder and are interested in finding out which security men were on duty here last Sunday night. Were Sam Leonard and Omar Fazal working here as doormen?'

'I don't know, love, they chop and change. Certainly two men came from Doormen Incorporated, but I can't say who they were,' June replied.

'Have you got CCTV here?' enquired Crawford.

'Yes,' she replied. 'For Sunday night you say? Sure, I'll get it for you. Do you want to watch it here?'

'If that's okay, I will,' said Crawford. 'It will move things on quicker. Can I go somewhere quieter?'

'Yes,' she said. 'Come with me,' and she took him upstairs to her flat.

'I'll put it on for you here, love. Sit here. Would you like a pint?' she asked.

'Not half. Thanks,' said Crawford as he sat down.

June brought the CDs to her flat where Crawford sat patiently watching the CCTV recording of the previous Sunday night's activities from 6:00 p.m. to 11:30 p.m. He was provided with a couple of pints of Timothy Taylors, which slipped down well. *If only it was always like this,* thought Crawford.

As he watched the tape, he saw that there were two doormen, but he couldn't make out if they were Leonard and Fazal as they were mostly out of sight.

Four hours into the tape it showed that at 10:00 p.m., a Rover 414 car pulled into the car park. *Bingo,* thought Crawford. From it emerged two men. They went into the pub. Crawford noted that 10:08 p.m. was just over two hours after the murder.

Crawford went down into the pub and asked June to come and look at the CCTV.

'Do you recognise these two?' he asked as he pointed to the two men.

'Yes,' she replied. 'They're Sam and Omar.'

Inside the pub, a second CCTV recording revealed that the man she had said was called Sam looked fidgety whilst the other one, she had identified as Omar, bought the drinks with a wad of money.

Nothing else of significance happened, so – after five and a half hours – he packed up the CCTV tapes and went back down into the pub to find June.

'Many thanks,' he said. 'I'll take the recordings if that's okay with you.'

'No problem,' she replied. 'They'd have been wiped tomorrow. You're welcome any time.'

'I'll take you up on that,' said Crawford. He signed a receipt for the tapes and left.

———•◦✦◦•———

Chapter 17
Omar Fazal's Arrest

Early the following morning, Turnbull and Jasper went to Omar Fazal's house in Sheffield, having got his address from his employers. It was a terrace house in a poor area. The small garden area to its front was overgrown, full of litter and food cartons.

A bleary-eyed man answered the door. 'What d'ya want at this time?' He was Asian, in his thirties, with a trim figure. He was about six feet tall and weighing about fourteen stones.

'Are you Omar Fazal?' Turnbull asked.

'Yes,' he replied.

'Can we come in?'

'I suppose so.'

'We're investigating a murder last Sunday night at about 8:00 p.m. on the moors between Halifax and Bradford. Where were you at that time?'

'I'm not sure. Probably working. I am a doorman with Doormen Incorporated.' His accent was broad Yorkshire.

'On Sundays, I usually work at the Rose and Crown here in Sheffield.'

'Well, were you there?'

'I've a memory like a sieve ... probably.'

'Have you ever been to the moors between Halifax and Bradford?'

'No.'

'Do you work with Sam Leonard?'

'Yes, we're always paired together.'

Turnbull told Fazal: 'We are arresting you for the murder of Mahmood Asgar last Sunday night at about eight o'clock on the moors between Bradford and Halifax.'

He was cautioned.

'Rubbish,' said Fazal. 'I've been expecting you and I've nothing to say until I've seen my solicitor.'

Turnbull asked for his mobile phone.

'Not sure where it is,' said Fazal. 'I keep losing it.'

He went in search, but Turnbull accompanied him to make sure he didn't try to flush it down the toilet. He found it in his bedroom and handed it over to D.I. Turnbull.

'Can you just take it like that?' asked Fazal.

'We have a court order from the Recorder of Bradford.'

'Okay,' replied Fazal.

Turnbull and Jasper then drove him to Bradford police station.

In the car, nothing was said.

At Bradford, he was put in a cell.

———•◦✷◦•———

Chapter 18
Asif Khan

Turnbull and Jasper next went, by appointment, to Armley Gaol in Leeds to see the residential governor, a lady called Jane Michaels. The prison had been built in red brick in Victorian times. It took twenty minutes to gain entry. Searches and x-rays delayed them.

'Thanks for seeing us,' Turnbull said to Jane Michaels. 'We're interested in a prisoner here called Wahid Mahmood. What can you tell us about him?'

'We've got nearly a thousand prisoners in here. I can't say I know him, but I'll send for his records. Do you want a cup of tea? We've run out of coffee.'

'Thanks.'

The records arrived, as did the tea, and Jane studied the file for a few minutes.

'He's a model prisoner,' she said. 'He's in here for an offence of supplying Class A drugs and is serving three-and-a-half years, allowing for good behaviour, he should be out in a year. What do you want him for?'

'We have strong reasons to believe he and his brother conspired with paid assassins to have his brother-in-law murdered,' replied Turnbull. 'We need to speak to anyone who shared a cell with him during the weeks leading up to the sixth of February, 2005; the day of the murder. He may have confided in his cellmate.'

'His records show that he shared a cell with a man called Asif Khan who's serving six years for blackmail,' said Jane. 'Khan has a history of deception and fraud so not, I would have thought, your most reliable witness. But then, who in this prison would be?'

'Can we speak to him?' asked Turnbull.

'Of course,' said the governor. 'I'll call for him now. By all means use this office. Wait here.'

Half an hour later, Asif Khan was brought into the room by a prison officer, to whom he was handcuffed. Turnbull guessed that Khan was in his thirties. His head was totally shaved and he was wearing prison clothes. He sat with the prison officer in the adjacent chairs.

Turnbull introduced himself and Jasper to Asif.

'You shared a cell with Wahid Mahmood in the weeks leading up to the sixth of February this year. He is believed to have organized, on the sixth of February, 2005, the murder in Halifax of Mahmood Asgar, his brother-in-law. Did you hear him say anything which might implicate him in that murder?'

'What's in it for me?' asked Asif.

Turnbull looked him in the eyes. 'I can't promise you anything, but a fellow Asian man was executed. He was shot in the back whilst kneeling down. One can hardly think of a more cowardly murder. Even villains, surely, have a code of conduct in this place.'

Asif said, 'Do you know what happens to a grass in here?'

'I can imagine,' replied Turnbull. 'But I wouldn't think a man who shot someone from behind when the victim was kneeling would have any respect, even in here. Do you want to think about it?'

'Okay, I'll think, but that's all.'

'Well, we'll come back tomorrow,' said Turnbull.

Asif said, 'Don't make it obvious. I don't want it to get around that I'm talking to the pigs.'

'Don't worry,' said Turnbull as Asif was taken out.

In the car on the way back to headquarters, Turnbull and Jasper discussed what had happened. 'I think he's going to tell us something,' Turnbull suggested.

'So do I,' said Jasper.

'As the boss said, Wahid may be a bragger who likes to impress his fellow in-mates. If he organised a murder, he likes power and to demonstrate it.

'Whether Asif dare say anything is a different matter. If his sentence is three-and-a-half years, with remission, he can't have long to serve. Jane said only one year. What's in it for him? Our only hope is that his conscience, if he has one, tells him to say something.'

'The problem is that cell confessions are looked on with great suspicion by lawyers and judges and, for all we know, by juries as well.

'Defence lawyers inevitably say how amazing it is that when evidence is thin, lo and behold, out of nowhere, comes a cell confession.'

They went to the pub for a quick drink and agreed Jasper would pick Turnbull up at eight the next morning.

Bang on eight, Jasper was at Turnbull's door. They drove through the rush hour to their second appointment with Asif.

Asif said, 'I did hear something. I submitted an application to see the prison liaison officer so I could tell him what I'd heard. No one came to see me so I thought "what the hell".'

'What did you hear that concerned you?' asked Turnbull.

'What protection will I get?'

'We'll do what we can, but no promises. It's make your mind up time. We're not coming back.'

'Alright, I did hear him talking to his brother, Nadeem, on a phone we had got illegally, and Wahid spoke to me after-wards about what Nadeem had said. He said that some guy was messing about with his sister and that the job would be sorted out in two weeks and that it would cost between five and £8,000.

'I was concerned about what he said because it sounded like

someone was going to get badly hurt. That's why I wanted to see the PLO, but no one came to see me. Burglary is one thing, but a severe beating is another. And he was Asian.'

'Let's start at the beginning,' said Turnbull. 'There's no hurry. You tell us how you knew Wahid and exactly what you heard him say and what he said to you.'

Asif continued, 'I'm from Halifax and I got to know a lot of people in the Asian community. One was Nadeem Khan. I used to go to his restaurant.

'Nadeem has two brothers. One is Wahid Mahmood, who I know is a heavy drug dealer at street level. He boasted to me of making seven grand a day. He has young Asian lads doing the running for him.

'In about December last year, I was moved into Wahid's cell here at Armley. We became friends. I'd got a mobile which had been smuggled into the prison. This is common. I said he could use it. Wahid said, if so, he would pay for it. It was a Panasonic flip phone with a Vodafone SIM card. We had it in the cell in what used to be a cupboard space that had been boarded up. We made a small hole so we would suspend the phone on a piece of string for easy access.

'How long did you have it for?' asked Turnbull.

'We had this phone for about three or four weeks and during that time I heard parts of conversations Wahid had with his brother Nadeem. After talking to his brother, Wahid would go quiet. I asked him what the problem was. He said, "Some guy is messing with my sister".'

'What else did he say?'

Asif continued, 'Wahid said, "We should have sorted it out when I was out. I told Nadeem to get the job done, we'll pay". He said the job would be sorted out in two weeks and would cost between five and £8,000.'

Turnbull thought that if that's right, the price has gone up from what Parveen told us.

'The phone was seized soon after. There was a disciplinary hearing before the governor. Wahid accepted responsibility for the phone and was given a twenty-one days suspended sentence.'

Turnbull said, 'We must seize that phone. Where is it?'

'It will be in a lock-up,' said Asif. By that he meant governor's custody.

Asif continued, 'Two days later, Wahid got another phone. It was a Sony Ericsson and it had two SIM cards. We both used it. Wahid used it to ring his brother. Wahid told me that Nadeem said the matter would be taken care of. Nadeem knew some people from Sheffield who would get the job done. Two were white and one was Asian. No names were mentioned.'

This fits, thought Turnbull, *with what I already know.*

'What happened next?' he asked.

'Then there was another search about two weeks later and the phone was seized. I took the blame for it and got the same sentence as Wahid. We were then put into different cells, but on the same wing.

'Some time later, I was in my cell watching the news, which reported that a man called Asgar had been shot near Halifax. After the news, I left my cell and was in the queue for our evening grub, when Wahid approached me and said, "Have you seen the news? The job's been done. It's our people who have done it".

'I thought, "a beating is one thing, but murder is something else".

'After this, he told me Nadeem had been arrested. Wahid asked me to telephone Nadeem and have him tell the police that he last saw Asgar in Pakistan and that he never visited Cardiff. I did as he said.'

'What number did you ring?'

'I remember the number I used, it ended in 333. I also remember using a number ending in 988.'

'What else did Wahid say?'

'Wahid also told me that he knew the place and he'd hidden seven ounces of crack in a wall near where the murder happened. He was worried that if the police recovered it, they might find his fingerprints on the wrapper.

'He also told me that Nadeem had been married to the Asian guy's sister and that they had split up. Later I remember Wahid saying to Nadeem, "We should have taken care of our sister as well. She brought disgrace on our family".'

'Anything else you can remember?'

'No.'

'Many thanks, Asif. Are you willing to give evidence of what you have said at trial?'

'I suppose so,' Asif replied. 'The poor sod didn't deserve to die. What had he done wrong?'

'He'd married their sister without their approval,' said Jasper.

'Okay,' said Turnbull. 'I'll speak to the governor about protection for you. Wahid needn't know for the moment that you've spoken to us. We'll see you again.'

Turnbull and Jasper left the prison and returned to their headquarters, buoyed up by their interview with Asif and hoping that he would stay safe. What he had said amounted to aiding and abetting the murder by Wahid.

However, they needed to recover the two phones which had been seized by the prison authorities, to check the numbers to see if they had been in contact with Nadeem. They also needed to examine the walls near the murder scene for crack cocaine and to find evidence which confirmed the accuracy of Asif's story. But why choose that spot to hide cocaine? It made little sense.

Turnbull knew that Asif would be regarded by the jury as an

unreliable witness who would think he would gain from giving this information. He had a bad record and so, without corroboration, would be regarded by the jury as of dubious quality.

'We need corroboration of his account,' Turnbull told Jasper. 'Let's hope the search reveals something. But even if it does, why was it there?'

———•••••———

The following day, Turnbull sent a search party to examine the wall near the scene of the murder. This party was independent of the investigation so that no allegations could be made, at trial, of planting evidence.

The search party worked in pairs so as to protect themselves against such an accusation.

After about an hour, a young police constable called Hawkyard noticed a large stone that had been loosened from its bed. He bent down, pulled it out and set it to the side. He put his hand in the hole and felt a smooth, cold plastic bag. He pulled it out and shouted, 'Bingo!' He called over the sergeant in charge. The bag was photographed, as was the hole. Inside the plastic bag was what looked like a drug of some sort. The bag was sent off to Wetherby for analysis.

On examination, it was found to contain nine ounces of crack cocaine but, unfortunately, no fingerprints were recovered from the bag.

At least they now had corroboration of part of Asif's account, but the chances were that Wahid's counsel would allege that the drugs had been planted, notwithstanding the precaution they had taken.

———•••••———

Chapter 19
Sam Leonard

Turnbull went, again, to see Leonard, who was still in custody and champing at the bit. His solicitor attended and sat down beside him.

Leonard said, 'You've got my DNA; I can't deny I was there, but I didn't pull the trigger. That's all I dare tell you. If I say any more, they'll get my family.'

Leonard was on the verge of tears and wringing his hands. He was sweating profusely.

'Who?' asked Turnbull.

'I can't tell you, it's more than my life's worth. I'm between the rock and a hard place.'

'You've no one to blame but yourself,' Turnbull told him.

This admission of presence at the scene by Leonard was, to Turnbull, a huge breakthrough. He thought that it was fanciful to think those intending to kill had taken with them a man, ignorant of the purpose of the trip, who might spill the beans.

Anyone in the car which had brought Asgar to the remote spot on the moors must surely have known what was intended. Otherwise, why take him? Unless it got out of hand.

Turnbull hoped that the telephone evidence would come up trumps.

Leonard was charged with the murder and made no reply.

———◆◆◆◆———

Chapter 20

The Arrest and Interviews of Nadeem, Wahid and Fazal

Turnbull and Jasper had put aside the day for the arrests of Nadeem, Wahid and Fazal.

It was a bleak morning and they set off for Halifax. They stopped at a coffee shop in Shelf for take-away coffees and enjoyed the steaming black liquid as they sat in the car.

'What do we expect of today?' asked Jasper.

'Not a lot, frankly, Dave,' said Turnbull. 'I can't see Nadeem or Wahid saying anything. They know our difficulty is connecting them with the Sheffield three. As for Fazal, he may be more forthcoming. He has put himself with Leonard at the time of the killing and we know Leonard was at the scene. If we can drive a wedge between Leonard and Fazal, all the better.'

Jasper drove slowly to Halifax in the mist and drizzle. Turnbull liked Halifax as a town. He remembered appearing, years ago, at Halifax Quarter Sessions as a witness before Altar Hurwitz, the Recorder of Halifax.

They arrived at Nadeem's restaurant. They knew he would be there because they had rung earlier. His solicitor, David Andrews, was with him. Turnbull knew him of old.

'Nadeem,' said Turnbull. 'Thank you for being here and you, Mr. Andrews. Is there anything new you wish to say, Nadeem?'

'No, I've told you. I know nothing of this murder and I've been advised to say nothing further.'

His solicitor confirmed that that was the case.

'Very well,' said Turnbull. 'Nadeem Khan, I am arresting you for the murder of Mahmood Asgar. You do not have to say anything, but it may harm your defence if you do not mention when questioned something you later rely on in court. Anything you say may be given in evidence. Do you understand?'

'Yes.'

'Well let's go. Are you going to follow on, Mr. Andrews?'

'Yes. I'll see you at Bradford headquarters. Can you arrange parking for me?'

'Sure,' said Jasper. 'Give me your registration number.'

They then set off in convoy to Bradford, down Manchester Road with its colourful Asian shops.

They went straight to the interview room, together with Mr. Andrews.

Nadeem was cautioned and opted, as he had been warned, to say nothing. He was then charged with the murder. He made no reply.

They then went their separate ways.

Nadeem was taken to the cells from where he would be taken to Leeds Prison as a remand prisoner. He may apply for bail, but it was rarely granted in murder cases.

Mr. Andrews returned to Halifax and Turnbull and Jasper went to the canteen for a coffee.

'How's your revision for your inspector's exam coming on?' asked Turnbull.

'Not bad, but we're so busy that I haven't had much spare time. But I guess it's the same for everyone.'

Turnbull liked Jasper. He had come up through the fast track; university and police college. He was unmarried and ambitious.

'Well, enough chat, let's get to Armley to see Wahid.'

They arrived at the prison and went through the usual rigmarole. Wahid's solicitor was already in the waiting area.

They were duly taken through to a huge room, divided into cubicles for interviews. Wahid was eventually brought in.

Wahid was cautioned and Turnbull said, 'You should know that we've spoken to one of your cellmates, Asif Khan, and he's told us about the telephone conversations you had with your brother, Nadeem, which he overheard. In which you and he planned the murder of your brother-in-law.'

'I should have known it was a mistake to share a cell with him. He's the most evil bastard in this prison. Do you know what he did?'

'Yes, we know.'

'You can't believe a word he says. He's after something.'

'Do you want to know what he says he overheard?' asked Turnbull.

'Not really. It will just make me angry. I wondered why he'd been moved from the prison. No doubt he's enjoying the easy life somewhere. But this will come back to bite him, you can be sure of that. Is it just his word?'

'Well, he said you had dealt in drugs at the scene of the murder and hidden some drugs in the wall. Lo and behold, we found drugs there.'

'Oh yeh? So now I'm selling drugs in winter on the moors. Not bloody likely. I'm a city boy. I don't go to the moors. It's too cold.'

'Did you know your sister was married?'

'Yes, but I had no problem with it, She's free to do what the hell she wants. I couldn't give a fuck what she does.'

'But how would he know there were drugs there unless you told him?'

'Maybe he put them there, or maybe you planted them. I wouldn't put it past you.'

'He says you mentioned Sheffield men as the killers and we believe the killers are from Sheffield. How would he know that?'

'Word gets around in this place. I bet this prison could solve half your cases.'

'So you say you never spoke to Asif about Nadeem or the murder of your sister-in-law?'

'Never. He's out for himself. I don't want to answer any more questions. If you're relying on Asif, you can't have much.'

'Well, Wahid, I'm now charging you with the murder of Asgar Mahmood.'

'I have nothing to say except don't rush back.'

Turnbull and Jasper left the prison and went to The Greyhound at Tong which was becoming a favourite spot for lunch. The two men sat at a copper-topped table with a pint each and a plate of sandwiches.

'What do you think, Dave?' asked Turnbull.

'Well, sir, the weakness is also the strength. The cocaine in the wall corroborates what Wahid said to Asif, but therein lies its weakness. I can't understand why a drug dealer would leave drugs in a wall on a moorland road. It's true that Asif couldn't have known of the Sheffield men unless he was told by Wahid. But Asif is such a shady character. Would you convict someone on his say so?'

'It will depend on how he comes across to the jury,' said Turnbull.

After lunch, they set off to see Omar Fazal. They rang to check he would be in and he told them he would stay at home and would expect them.

Again they trailed down the M1 to Sheffield. When they arrived at Fazal's house, they were surprised to find him there with a solicitor called Ahmed.

'Good of you to be in and thanks, Mr. Ahmed, for being here,' said Turnbull.

'We've just arrested Sam Leonard, Nadeem Khan and Wahid Mahmood for the murder of Mahmood Asgar. You will appreciate that we intend to arrest you, Omar Fazal, for the same offence, which I now do.

'You do not have to say anything, but it may harm your defence if you do not mention when questioned something you later rely on in court. Anything you say may be given in evidence. I assume, Mr. Ahmed, that you have explained that to your client.'

'Yes and he has no reply.'

'Fair enough,' said Turnbull. 'Is there anything you wish to say, Omar?'

'Yes. I work as a doorman on most Friday, Saturday and Sunday nights. I don't know about that particular night. I worked with Sam Leonard. I didn't leave Sheffield last Sunday. At about five or six o'clock, I went to my girlfriend's house. She's called Sandra Jaimes. Then, later that evening, we went to Sam's house coz Sandra wanted to see Sam's wife.

'Sam and I left the two girls while we went to the Rose and Crown coz someone owed me money. After that, we went back to Sam's, and Sandra and I went home.'

'Did you or Sam telephone your employer to say you weren't going to work that night?'

'No.'

'Finally, do you know a man called Jack Rastrick?'

'Yes, he's a doorman as well.'

That's the connection, thought Turnbull. *We may now have the three assassins.*

Omar Fazal was then charged with the murder of Mahmood Asgar and made no reply.

They took him back to Bradford.

Turnbull and Jasper realized that Fazal's account now fitted with the video evidence of the two men at the pub.

Nadeem was arrested for a second time and re-interviewed. He denied any knowledge of the three Sheffield men.

Nadeem was charged with the murder and replied "Not guilty".

Chapter 21
Sandra Jaimes

The following morning, Turnbull and Jasper went to see Sandra Jaimes to see whether she confirmed Omar Fazal's alibi for the time of the murder. Turnbull was used to false alibis being raised by partners and was deeply suspicious of them.

He and Jasper found Sandra at her home in Sheffield. She lived in a terrace house on a street of red brick houses.

A young woman in her thirties answered the door. She looked weary, as if she carried the worries of the world on her shoulders.

'Are you Sandra Jaimes?' Turnbull asked.

'Who wants to know?' she replied.

'We're police officers from Bradford. We've come to see you about Omar Fazal. We understand you go out together,' said Turnbull.

'Yes,' she answered. 'For several years now. Come in.' They were taken into the living room. 'Would you like some tea?' she asked.

'Yes, please. Nice house you have here,' said Turnbull, and it was – freshly painted with tasteful prints on the wall and a warm, flame gas fire in the living room. She obviously took pride in her home. Turnbull wondered how a nice woman like her could get involved with a man like Omar Fazal.

'I understand you know Omar Fazal?'

'Yes, I've known him over ten years. We are good friends. Well, I suppose, more than that. You know what I mean,' she replied.

'What about Sam Leonard?' asked Turnbull. 'Do you know him?'

'Yes, and his wife, Suzanne. She's my mate. I used to work at a nightclub and Sam used to be its security guard.'

'We're interested in Omar's movements last Sunday night at about eight o'clock. Did you see him that night?'

'Yes, I think that's when we went away for a weekend in Blackpool. We stayed in a B&B.'

'Who booked it?'

'Omar did.'

'Have you got a receipt?'

'No.'

'Could you give us the address?'

'No, Omar will know it.'

'Did you go by train or car?'

'Car.'

'Whose?'

'His.'

'That's odd, because he says that last Sunday night you both went to Sam's.'

'He must be confused. As far as I remember, we went to Blackpool.'

'It's not that long since; surely you know whether you were in Blackpool or at Sam's.'

'You're getting me confused, or Omar's confused.'

'We believe he was involved in a murder last Sunday night in Halifax.'

'Not Omar, he would never do anything like that.'

'Well, you'd better think about it. I assume you know that assisting a murderer is, in itself, a very serious offence.'

'Look, I'm not assisting any murderer. I don't like your insinuations.'

'Think about it. We'll see you again,' said Turnbull.

He and Jasper then left.

James thought, *how could they make such a mess of*

organising an alibi? She should be easy to break down. We'll go early in the morning.

The following morning, Turnbull and Jasper returned to Sandra's house.

By now they were bored with these journeys to Sheffield. They listened to Radio 4.

Sandra let them in and immediately said, 'Look, I don't want any trouble. Tell me again what he's meant to have done.'

'A man was shot in the back and killed on the moors near Halifax. We believe Omar was there when it happened. Whether or not he pulled the trigger, we don't know. But he was there with Sam Leonard.'

'Look, Omar's no murderer. If he was there, it wouldn't be him who shot anyone. He wouldn't hurt a fly.' She fiddled with a piece of paper.

'Look, you're badgering me. All I know is, he didn't murder anyone.'

'Well,' said Turnbull. 'If it happened without him having any foresight of a plan to kill, it's just possible he wouldn't be guilty of murder. What we're trying to establish is whether he was there or not.'

'Look,' said Sandra, 'he's terrified of being accused of murder if he was there and knew nothing.'

'So, was he there or not?' asked Turnbull.

'Okay. Last Saturday night he came here and said he needed an alibi for the following night.'

'What for?'

'He didn't say, but not for any murder, for God's sake.'

'What exactly did he say?'

'Look, I love the guy. I don't want him in any trouble coz of me.'

'Well, what did he say?'

'He said if the police were to ask where he was on the

evening of Sunday, sixth of February, I should tell them we went away for the weekend together. Later, he came to see me. He was very uptight. I asked why he wanted me to alibi for him for the sixth of February and he said he had driven to Halifax where a man had been picked up. The man had been shot. Omar had been the driver. He didn't say who he was with.'

Turnbull reduced what she said to writing in his notebook and asked her to sign it – which she did.

What a turn up, thought Turnbull. *Let's now see whether we make similar progress with Jack Rastrick.*

Turnbull worried that Sandra Jaimes would go back on her statement at trial, as would Parveen, and that it would be messy.

Chapter 22
Jack Rastrick

James Turnbull was in his office in Bradford looking out of the window at the old Gaumont Cinema, remembering the day he saw the Beatles perform there, when Dave Jasper came rushing in from the corridor.

'You won't believe what I've found out,' he said.

'Wahid has confessed that he set it up?' suggested Turnbull.

'No, not quite as good as that, but nearly. Guess where Jack Rastrick is at the moment.'

'Marbella?'

'No, one more guess.'

'Gibraltar?'

'No, he's in Armley gaol.'

'You're not saying he was there when the murder was committed, are you?'

'No, much better than that. He's been arrested for involvement in a shooting in Sheffield on the twentieth of February, fourteen days after our shooting.'

'In what circumstances?'

'You won't believe the similarities. A curry delivery boy was called to deliver at a spot in Sheffield and was shot seven times with a handgun.'

'What type of handgun?'

'One the exact replica of the one used to shoot Asgar.'

'Bingo,' said Turnbull. 'That shows a propensity to act in this way. The judge in our trial may allow the second shooting in evidence as it bears striking similarities to ours.'

'Exactly,' said Jasper. 'And we know where to find him.'

'If the second shooting goes in evidence, he'll be dead in the water. I'm amazed he used his own telephone to ring Joe Ogden.'

'Well, he would never have dreamt that Sam's DNA would be found on a cigarette tab at the scene. Think where we would've been without that evidence. The brothers wouldn't have said anything. Oh, thank God for the miracles of science.'

'We'll go and see him tomorrow,' said Turnbull. 'Ring Jane Michaels and set it up.'

'I think she fancies you,' said Jasper.

'Go along with you,' said Turnbull.

The following morning, they met with Jane in her office.

'I gather that, this time, you want to see Jack Rastrick. A naughty boy is our Jack. I've had his file brought up for you. He's awaiting trial for attempted murder by shooting.'

'We know,' said Turnbull. 'Can we see him?'

'He's on his way, but he's a Grade A prisoner, so you'll have to see him in a more secure spot than here.'

She took them down the corridor to a secure interview room. Rastrick was seated at a table, with prison officers on either side of him.

'Well, Jack,' said Turnbull. 'Do you know why we're here? We're from the Bradford homicide squad and we believe you were involved in the shooting of one Mahmood Asgar, on the sixth of February, on the moors outside Halifax.'

'Piss off,' said Rastrick. 'I'm not answering any questions.'

And that was that.

Turnbull thanked the governor for her help and he and Jasper left.

Enquiries made at the council offices revealed that, according to the electoral register, also living at Rastrick's address was one Helen Munro. Probably Rastrick's partner, they thought.

'Let's see what she has to say,' said Turnbull.

Chapter 23

Helen Munro

The Rastrick house was near Fazal's and very similar in appearance.

Turnbull and Jasper arrived there early to be sure she was in. They couldn't call beforehand because there was no landline telephone. They rang the bell and a woman answered the door.

'Yes?' she said.

'We're police officers from Bradford,' said Turnbull as both he and Jasper showed her their warrant cards. 'Do you mind if we ask you a few questions?'

'I suppose not. Come in.'

Helen was in her late thirties, with a good figure. She was quite tall, about five nine, with dark hair. She was smartly dressed in tight jeans and a white silk shirt.

They followed her into the living room. Turnbull was surprised how lavish their living quarters were. There was a huge flat-screen television on the wall, a modern hi-fi system and a drinks cabinet.

How does a man on security guard's pay afford all this, pondered Turnbull. *Maybe she has a good job and she's the bread winner.*

'We're sorry to disturb you, but we have some questions about Jack Rastrick,' said Turnbull.

'Well, you know where he is. He's in Armley awaiting trial for attempted murder. Bloody fool. Why does he get mixed up in this business? He doesn't need to. He has a good job and I'm a medical secretary. Between us we have a good living, thank you, and no dependents.'

'Is he pleading guilty, or not guilty?' asked Turnbull.

'I think he's banged to rights, as they say, and will be pleading guilty.'

'What's your relationship?'

'We are partners in every sense.'

'How did you come to be together?'

'A chance meeting. He's rough, but very attractive. I suppose it was animal lust. I just fell for him.'

'Fair enough. I'm afraid he may well be involved in another shooting.'

'Oh, God, no. What is it this time?'

'A shooting on the moors outside Halifax. The victim is dead.'

Helen went pale. 'I thought there was still a chance for us after he'd served his sentence for the attempt offence, but if what you say is true, this looks like the end for us.'

Jasper went to the kitchen and got her a glass of water.

'So, how can I help you?' Helen asked.

'Have you visited him whilst he's been on remand?'

'Yes, of course, as often as possible.'

'Has he said anything about this other shooting on the eleventh of February?

'No, he said nothing.'

'Well, Helen, my instincts tell me that he spoke to you about it. Villains often brag about their offending or want to confide in someone. He must have heard through the grapevine of the arrest of Omar Fazal and Sam Leonard. He would be worried that we would come to him as the third man and would want to confide in you.

'We know he bought a car and, shortly after the killing, it was found burnt out. The reason it was destroyed is because it had been used to take him, Leonard and Fazal to Halifax to take the victim up to the moors where he was shot in the back as he knelt down. In other words, an execution.

'We don't know which of the three shot him, or who the driver was, but Jack was one of the three.'

'Well, I know nothing about that.'

'Where was he last Sunday night?'

'I can't remember.'

'It's only last Sunday we're talking about.'

'I don't want to say any more. I will go today to see my solicitor after work.'

'Well, you do that. He's a loser and not worth helping.'

'Will you go now, please?'

'Yes. Can we have your mobile number, please?'

'Yes, I'll write it down for you.'

'Will you please ring me when you've seen your solicitor. Here's my card,' said Turnbull.

'Yes, I will, tomorrow. Will you go now, please?'

'Of course. My advice would be not to go to see him,' said Turnbull and he and Jasper left.

On the journey back, Jasper said, 'I don't know whether she'll come across. She's brighter than Sandra Jaimes. She's no future with Rastrick. She's an attractive woman. She should wash her hands of him, but I don't know whether she will.'

'I agree,' said Turnbull. 'But women are unpredictable, as we all know. Let's see what she says after seeing her solicitor.'

Early the following day, Turnbull was in his office. He had come in early to avoid the traffic on Canal Road into Forster Square which, any later, would have proved horrendous. He planned on working in his office until Helen Munro rang him and then going to Sheffield.

Jasper was out of the office working with Jane on the telephone evidence.

Turnbull's phone rang at 1:10 p.m.

'Mr Turnbull, it's Helen Munro here. I'm ready to continue

our conversation.'

'Excellent,' said Turnbull. 'Will three o'clock this afternoon be convenient?'

'Can you make it 4:30? I am usually at work until five, but my boss has agreed to let me leave at four.'

'Fair enough. 4:30 p.m. it is then, at your house.'

'However,' said Helen, 'you should know that the position is as before. He said he had nothing to do with any murder.'

'We'll still come and see you,' said Turnbull.

Jasper returned from working with Jane and drove the two of them to Sheffield in the dusk.

Helen let them in. She was wearing a dark suit, a necktie and high heels. *Very smart,* thought Turnbull.

She said, 'I've told you on the phone, he said nothing to me about any murder.'

'Helen,' said Turnbull. 'If you're afraid, he can't get at you himself. He'll get at least ten years for the attempt and a minimum of over twenty for the shooting on the sixth of February, so I wouldn't think you're in any danger from him.

'The alternative is to lie for him, which could get you into serious trouble. What is it to be?'

'He said nothing,' she said.

'Okay,' said Turnbull. 'I'm sure you won't, but it would be better if you didn't see him again.'

'Alright, but I just find it so hard.'

They left her thinking she would see him and would talk to him about what they'd said to her.

Turnbull and Jasper then left.

They then went to The Greyhound at Tong. Turnbull got them a beer and some port scratchings. The pub had just opened and it was too early for lunch.

'I've had an idea,' said Turnbull. 'Helen Munro isn't going to drop Rastrick in it. She wouldn't dare, and she's a different kettle of fish to Sandra Jaimes. However, she's bound to go and see him whatever we say and, with a bit of luck, she'll tell him about our visits. He may then spill the beans and say he was at the scene of the murder, but he may say, as we expect all three to say, that he wasn't the shooter and was taken by surprise. But presence is enough for us.'

'But how will we know what is said?' asked Jasper.

'Well,' said Turnbull. 'I think we may be able to bug the conversation.'

'Will the prison let us do that?'

'It's been done before,' said Turnbull. 'I was at a senior officers' conference recently and we were told that, in a recent case, the Court of Appeal said evidence called in trial of a bugged conversation was properly admitted. True, it was in a police cell and not a prison, but I can't see what difference that would make. Let's see if Jane Michaels will allow the cell to be bugged when Helen next visits Jack Rastrick.'

'What a brilliant idea. Do you think she'll wear it?

'No harm in trying. Let's have another half.'

————◆◆◆◆————

Back at the police station, Turnbull rang Jane Michaels and said what he proposed.

'I don't know,' she said. 'I'll have to get Home Office approval.'

'See what you can do and ring me here.' He gave her his direct line.

'Will do,' said Jane.

Three hours later, Jane rang back. Turnbull was still in his office.

'I've got approval from the Home Office on-site lawyer.

I've also spoken to the senior governor here and he's willing to give it a go, although he thinks that any such evidence would breach the right to privacy under human rights law.'

'Well, it's worth a try,' said Turnbull.

'Okay,' said Jane. 'I'll check when she's next due to visit him and if you send your tech people here, I'll arrange for a specific cubicle to be set aside for them to bug.'

'Excellent,' said Turnbull. 'Many thanks again. You're terrific.'

'No probs,' said Jane.

<hr />

Helen Munro visited Rastrick three days later. She sat in the cubicle waiting for him to be brought in. He arrived and sat in the cubicle opposite her whilst the prison officer sat outside.

When they were alone, Helen said, 'What the hell have you being doing? As if one attempted murder is not enough, you've now gone and done it, you've murdered someone. This is the end, Jack, I can't stand any more.'

'No, that's not fair. I haven't murdered anyone.'

'Oh, no, what were you doing in Halifax on the sixth of February?'

'Yes, I went to Halifax with two others, but I didn't shoot the man, one of the others did.'

'You know as well as I do, Jack, that if you were there with the others, you will be held responsible. Don't play the innocent with me. Why go in the first place?'

'They said they were going to teach him a lesson, rough him up a bit, not kill him.'

'Well, why did they kill him?'

'One went nuts. He said the man knew we were from Sheffield and so he just killed him.'

'Why didn't you stop him?'

'Look, whose side are you on?'

'Not yours, Jack, I've had enough.' And with that she walked out of the cubicle leaving Rastrick open-mouthed.

———————

Turnbull and Jasper put down their headphones. They were in Jane Michaels' office. 'Bingo, we've got him,' said Turnbull. He went to Jane and gave her a hug.

'Steady on,' she said.

———————

The following day they returned to see Rastrick at Leeds prison. This time, in the presence of his solicitor from T I Clough in Bradford, whom Turnbull knew from old. Desmond Joyce was well known throughout the criminal fraternity.

Turnbull confronted Rastrick with the taped conversation and asked him whether he wanted to say anything.

Rastrick immediately said, 'Alright, I admit I drove them there but, honest, I had no idea they were going to murder the man.'

Turnbull said, 'You're saying they took you with them without your knowing the purpose of the visit? That doesn't ring true. Why take you at all. You may have blabbed and then could be a witness against them. And you're in custody for an almost identical shooting two weeks later and with a gun of the same make. You are a hired gunman. You kill for money.'

'I'm saying nothing else,' said Rastrick.

Turnbull and Jasper then took their leave and went back to Sheffield to search Rastrick's house.

A surprised Helen Munro was still there.

'Not expecting you again,' she said.

'Well, we now want to conduct a search to see if there is anything here to connect Jack with the journey to Halifax.'

In his hallway, they found a yellow fluorescent jacket with stripes. This was sent to the Forensic Science Laboratory in Wetherby. From one of the sleeves, a miniscule amount of firearm residue was recovered.

Chapter 24

Another Case Conference

On the Tuesday, ten days after the murder, Detective Superintendent Illingworth called a case conference at Bradford C.I.D. HQ. This time, a Solicitor from the Crime Prosecution Service was present, together with Illingworth, Turnbull, Jasper, Oddy and Jane Rowley.

'James, tell us how things stand against each of the five men you've arrested.'

'Well,' said Turnbull. 'The case against Leonard, Fazal and Rastrick is the easiest to prove.

'We know that Leonard was present from the DNA recovered from the cigarette butt left at the scene. He's admitted such, but denied participation. I see little problem in proving his involvement on a joint-enterprise basis. Those who took Asgar to the scene, intending to kill him, are each guilty of murder.

'I doubt whether Leonard will enter the witness box as, if he does, he's bound to incriminate at least his two confederates and possibly also the two brothers who conscripted him. His telephone use also establishes complicity as you will hear from Jane.

'Omar Fazal is not so straight forward. He was with Leonard on the night of the murder. He was seen arriving at the Rose and Crown with him, after the murder, and they were in the Rover which was later found burnt out. And CCTV footage, from the Rose and Crown, shows him paying for drinks with a wad of money in his hand. He asked his girlfriend, Sandra Jaimes, to give him a false alibi for the night in question. He admitted to her that he went to Halifax with the other two, but was totally shocked when Leonard shot Asgar.

'His likely defence, as for all of them, is presence but not participation.

'As for Rastrick, he bought the car which we believe was used in the murder, which was burnt out hours after the killing. He confessed to his girlfriend, Helen Munro, that he was present at the scene, but denies knowledge in advance of what was to happen.

'There may be argument at the trial that the taped conversation is not admissible in evidence. However, I doubt it would succeed.

'The girlfriend of Fazal will probably go back on her witness statement, which implicates him, through fear of reprisals. That problem will have to be handled at trial, if it arises.

'The case against the two brothers is more difficult. The Sheffield assassins had themselves no motive to kill, so they were conscripted for money by others.

'A key witness against them is their sister, Parveen. She is between a rock and a hard place. She will go back on her statement or allege we put her up to it. I reckon she will be treated by the judge as a witness hostile to the Crown's case and her witness statement will be admitted in evidence.

'It will then be for the jury to decide what they believe, if anything, of what she said. The defence will have a field day with her.

'Telephone evidence connects Nadeem to the killers, as you will hear.

'The case against Wahid is the more difficult because he was in prison at the time of the murder. Asif Khan shared a cell with him and Wahid confessed to him his involvement. But Asif is a villain himself and his credibility is on the line. Also, we don't know whether he will come up to proof at trial and give evidence in accordance with what he has said to us.

'Crack cocaine has been found in a bag hidden in the wall

near to the scene of the killing, so this corroborates Asif's story. But what was it doing there? The jury may be reluctant to convict a man of murder who was in prison when it was committed and against whom the main evidence is a cell confession to a villain.

'That's about it, Gov, we'll have to play it by ear.'

'Thanks for that,' said Illingworth. 'Now, Jane, tell us what your research into the telephones reveals.'

'Well, sir, it confirms contact between the two brothers and the three alleged assassins, and presence at the scene.

'However, it appears from what D.I. Turnbull has said that presence at the scene is not disputed by the three alleged assassins.

'However, this is what I have found out.

'We have the telephones of all the accused, including two phones from the prison.

'The telephone number on the van outside Leonard's house was Leonard's and that number was used to telephone Nadeem's home in Parkinson Lane, Halifax.

'Also, within the memory of Nadeem's phone, were two numbers stored as Faz1 and Faz2. So this confirms contact between Leonard and Nadeem, and Nadeem and Fazal.

'Also, one of the phones recovered from the prison was used to ring Leonard's number. So that confirms contact between Wahid and Leonard.

'Also, days before the murder, Fazal's phone was used to ring Nadeem's number, and Wahid's prison phone was used the same day to ring the deceased, Asgar's, phone. So that confirms contact between Fazal and Nadeem; and between Wahid and Asgar.

'Obviously, we don't know what was said in any of these telephone calls, but the phone evidence is consistent with our case that the two brothers conscripted the three Sheffield men. It's also some confirmation of Parveen's account that Asgar received threatening calls from her brothers.

'Rastrick's phone was used to ring Fazal, and Fazal's phone was used to ring Leonard. Rastrick's phone was also used to ring the car owner, Joe Ogden. So that confirms contact between the three killers; and the acquisition by Rastrick of the car used in the killing.

'Finally, there was silence between all five from the time the car was bought on the Friday afternoon until after the murder, which is consistent with the three men being together at the time of the killing and not in need of speaking to each other by telephone.

'All in all, it fits with our case.'

'Thank you, Jane, and well done. I know how painstaking such research is. Print out the calls from the different numbers and highlight the ones you have referred to.

'Well, everyone, it looks as though the case against Wahid is the weakest. We'll have to hope Asif comes across well as a witness.

'The next stage is to organize a consultation with counsel.'

Chapter 25

Crown Prosecution Service
Case Conference

The Crown Prosecution Service (CPS) organized a case conference at Prosecuting Counsel's Chambers, in Leeds, four weeks before the trial. Present were the two prosecuting counsel, plus James Turnbull and Dave Jasper. The CPS representative, Myles Gibson, a very experienced court legal executive, but not a qualified solicitor, was also present. He would be in court, sitting behind prosecuting counsel.

Turnbull always found the conference room impressive. A huge oblong mahogany table with a dozen or so chairs, a high ceiling and a magnificent chandelier. Papers and pencils were placed on the table in front of each seat. The walls were covered with paintings of Leeds and cartoon pictures of judges from years past.

'Thank you for coming,' said Tom Beecroft, Q.C., leading counsel for the prosecution. 'This is Jeff Oldroyd, my junior. He is very experienced and knows the case backwards. Please sit down.' They were served coffee.

Tom Beecroft was, thought Turnbull, about forty-five. He wore a plain, grey suit and a red bow tie. He was slightly overweight and had a ready smile. Jeff Oldroyd, on the other hand, was only in his twenties and very smartly dressed in pinstriped trousers and a black jacket.

'We think the prosecution case has been well investigated and researched,' said Beecroft. 'I have read the notes of your last case conference, so I don't need to go over old ground. As against the two brothers, a lot will depend on how Parveen comes across as a witness and what tack she takes.

'The most likely recruiters were the family, so common sense supports her version. We decided not to pursue the father as the case against him is weak. The most we could prove would be knowledge. As far as we know, he took no active part. The same with the mother. They just sat back and did nothing.'

Jeff Oldroyd said, 'I have done schedules and a flowchart showing the interaction of the various telephones. Based upon excellent work by Detective Jane Rowley, we need stills showing what we believe is the car used in the murder nearing the deceased's house and leaving in the direction of the murder site.

'We are preparing a bundle for each pair of jurors, the witness box and the judge. The bundle should include maps showing the various points of importance: the deceased's house; Parveen and her brothers' home; the restaurant. Then the Sheffield end; the defendants' homes; the Rose and Crown; the location of the burnt-out car; the route to Halifax. You know the score.'

'Defence statements have been put in by all five defendants,' Beecroft said. 'Leonard is the only one who, in his defence statement, has admitted presence. The other two Sheffield men have denied presence and have put forward an alibi. The brothers denied incitement to murder.

'This surprises me as the evidence points to Rastrik and Fazaal's presence. I expected a defence of non-participation. But there we go. How is Parveen?'

Myles Gibson replied, 'She has recently been to a solicitor and made a statement retracting almost everything she said to us. She went back to live with the family.'

He handed out copies of the retraction statement.

'Her explanation for what she says are earlier lies is that she thought that, because of what her in-laws said, it must be her brothers and so she lied, implicating them. They have now persuaded her that they had nothing to do with it.'

'That's par for the course,' said Beecroft. 'I doubt whether any defendant will give evidence. We'll see soon enough. Parveen won't be able to explain how she came to make her statement implicating her brothers before she even spoke to her in-laws.'

'We agree,' said Turnbull.

'Okay,' said Beecroft. 'I think that covers everything. Thank you all for coming.'

Chapter 26
The Trial

The trial was set down at Teesside Crown Court, chosen by the Presiding Judge of the North Eastern Circuit so as to be as far away as possible from the locality in which the murder was committed, but within the North Eastern Circuit.

The case had attracted enormous publicity in the Bradford region. The local paper, the *Telegraph & Argus*, had condemned the practice of honour killing, which presupposed the family was behind it and so it was thought the brothers would not get a fair trial in Bradford.

The judge was Mr Justice Griffiths, a former London criminal practitioner, well-versed in the intricacies of a long murder trial. He was staying in the judges' lodgings in nearby Kirkleavington.

'All stand,' called out the usher as the red-gowned and wigged high court judge shuffled into court. He looked young, thought Turnbull, but so did most people these days.

The court was full. In the press box were the usual journalists plus, Turnbull guessed, some from London. In the public gallery were a lot of Asian faces, presumably up from Bradford, and the occasional white face of the regular spectators.

The judge addressed counsel, 'I take it all defendants speak English so that there is no need for an interpreter.'

Counsel, in turn, agreed that it was unnecessary.

'Will the defendants please stand,' ordered the clerk of the court from his position below the judge.

'Nadeem Khan, Wahid Mahmood, Sam Leonard, Omar Fazal and Jack Rastrick – each of you is charged with murder and the particulars are that on the sixth of February 2005, in

Halifax, you murdered Mahmood Asgar. How do you plead –
guilty or not guilty?'

Nadeem Khan replied, 'Not guilty.'

Wahid Mahmood replied, 'Not guilty.'

Sam Leonard replied, 'Not guilty.'

Omar Fazal replied, 'Not guilty.'

Jack Rastrick replied, 'Not guilty.'

The defendants looked calm and relaxed behind the glass
screen in Teesside's relatively new court building.

The judge addressed the thirty or so jurors-in-waiting who
were sitting patiently at the back of the court. 'Good morning
ladies and gentlemen. Twelve of you will try these five men,
each of whom is alleged to have murdered Mahmood Asgar.

'The trial is estimated to last several weeks or thereabouts.
I know you were told your stint would last about two weeks,
but you were also told that some cases take longer. This is one
such case.

'If any of you, when called to sit as a juror, has a press-
ing reason why you cannot sit for five weeks or so, you can
approach me and tell me, and I will decide whether to excuse
you from acting as a juror in this trial.'

The court clerk then called out the names of the jurors one
by one. Four approached the bench and the judge made his
decision,

Turnbull thought, after four intelligent-looking jurors had
been excused, *We now have twelve unemployed jurors. Let's
hope they understand what's going on.*

He recalled a fraud trial at Sheffield Crown Court which
took place during Sheffield holiday week when he thought none
of the jury could afford a holiday. However, in his view, their
verdicts were right in the end. Common sense is the greatest
virtue in a jury.

When the twelve were in the jury box, they were put in

charge by the court clerk. In other words, each taking an oath to try each of the defendants according to the evidence. The verdicts now had to be the jury's, no one else's.

The waiting jurors, those not sworn, were then released.

'Yes, Mr Beecroft,' said the judge, indicating that he should begin his opening speech.

Tom Beecroft, Q.C., leading counsel for the prosecution, then began his opening speech to the jury. He was at the end of the front row of leading counsel (Queen's Counsel) with their juniors seated behind them. Beecroft had a lectern on which to rest his papers.

The jury was a mixed bunch. One Afro-Caribbean woman, two Asian men and the rest a mix of ages and sexes from Middlesbrough.

As Beecroft began, there was total silence and an air of anticipation in the court.

'Ladies and gentlemen of the jury, on Sunday, the sixth of February 2005, at about 8:00 p.m., John and Janet Abbott were driving home from a lunch at the Goose Inn at Ogden. They'd enjoyed roast beef and Yorkshire pudding and a couple of drinks. Their route took them over the moors between Bradford and Halifax, a journey they knew well and which avoided main roads.

'As John approached a junction on his left, a car suddenly emerged. He had to brake hard to avoid a collision. The car moved back to allow them to pass, but as they passed the junction, Janet thought she saw a body in the road behind the car.

'The car then moved out and followed them.

'As he approached another junction, John turned off and let the car continue on its way.

'They returned to the first junction and there they found the body of a man lying in the road. He had been shot in the back. An ambulance was called and he was taken to Halifax Hospital.

He was pronounced dead at 4:00 a.m. the following day.

'The trial is about the dead man's murder. Who shot him and why? It certainly wasn't a robbery. He had £30 in cash on him when he was found.

'The prosecution's case is that the man was killed to order. Those present at the scene and responsible for the shooting were Sam Leonard, Omar Fazal and Jack Rastrick. But they were not acting on their own initiative. They had been recruited to do the job by Nadeem Khan and Wahid Mahmood.

'Please look in the bundle before you. You will see the indictment, at page one, the charge that you are trying.

'All five defendants are charged with murder. The defendants are represented as follows:

'Nadeem Khan by my learned friend Miss Davies Q.C. and Mr Dodds.

'Wahid Mahmood by my learned friend Mr Archbold Q.C. and Miss Wadham.

'Sam Leonard by my learned friend Mr May Q.C. and Miss McLean.

'Omar Fazal by my learned friend Mr Stewart Q.C. and Mr Batty.

'Jack Rastrick by my learned friend Mr Mountfield Q.C. and Mr Blackstone.

'I appear with Mr Oldroyd for the prosecution. It will be our duty to call the evidence before you but before doing so, I will tell you something about the case and the evidence that I anticipate you will hear. This should assist you in understanding how the evidence fits together.

'That a murder took place is unlikely to be disputed.

'You will be concerned with the identities of the men who committed the murder.

'The prosecution say that the five men in the dock committed the murder.

'What evidence will the prosecution call before you which will establish the guilt of these five men?

'Firstly, direct evidence of the involvement of these men and, secondly, evidence of circumstances which point to their involvement.

'The direct evidence comes from three sources.

'Eye-witness evidence, such as the Abbotts', who saw the aftermath of the shooting.

'Evidence that the men in the dock have spoken about or admitted their roles to friends and associates.

'In the case of Sam Leonard, evidence of certain admissions to the police. Also, he smoked a cigarette at the scene and from the tab-end, his DNA has been recovered.

'The prosecution also relies upon evidence of various circumstances relating to the crime and individual defendants which, when taken together, will lead you to the sure conclusion that each is guilty of murder.

'Thus, in addition, you will hear other evidence of the behaviour of the defendants before and after the murder.

'Evidence of experts linking Sam Leonard to the scene and identifying a car seen on CCTV making its way to the scene of the murder. The car was purchased by Jack Rastrick in the hours before the murder.

'Evidence of telephone contact indicating they had a common purpose.'

Mr Beecroft then went on to tell the jury about the deceased, Mahmood Asgar, his history, his meeting Parveen and the threats. He told them about Parveen, her history, her meeting Mahmood, of her marriage, her husband's arrival in the United Kingdom and of his life in hiding until his death.

He moved on to the Sheffield accused, the purchase of the car, the murder scene, the science, the tracing of the leisure card. Finally, he told them about Asif Khan and his conversations with Wahid, about the telephone evidence, the interviews and the arrests, the evidence of the girlfriends. He went on …

'What are the issues you will have to consider in this trial? Nadeem and Wahid deny any involvement in, or knowledge of, this murder. The question for you is whether, contrary to their denials, you can be sure that these two brothers were involved in some way in commissioning this murder; in procuring the Sheffield men to shoot Mahmood Asgar. Provided you are sure they were involved, each is guilty of murder.

'Omar Fazal and Jack Rastrick deny any knowledge or participation in the murder. The issue for you is whether you are sure they were involved.

'Sam Leonard, faced with the matching DNA profile, has admitted being present at the killing, but he too denies participation.

'In conclusion, you will want to bear in mind the principal upon which you should act is that the prosecution has brought the charges and the burden of proof is throughout on the prosecution.

'You will also bear in mind that the standard of proof is such that before you can convict any defendant, you must be sure of his guilt.

'You must consider each defendant separately. The prosecution's case is that they committed this murder together.

'Where a criminal offence is committed by two or more persons, each may play a different role, but if they are in it together, as part of a joint plan or agreement to commit it, each is guilty.

'And so it would not matter that a particular defendant could not be shown to have fired the gun. No one in this trial may ever admit firing the gun. However, provided you are satisfied that the shooting was carried out as part of a joint plan, then it matters not that one defendant may have fired the shot, another may have been an organiser, another a driver or another simply there to lend a hand. If they were all involved as part of a joint plan then each is guilty.'

'We'll adjourn now for lunch,' said the judge. 'Throughout this case you, the jury, must not speak to another outside your number about this case or allow another to speak to you about it. The reason is that you reach your verdicts on the evidence you hear in this court and on no other basis.'

The jury withdrew.

The judge then rose, as did those in court who bowed and he bowed back. He then withdrew.

'That was a good opening,' Turnbull said to Jasper, 'Clear, concise and powerful. Let's go for a bite to eat.'

The two men went to a pub James knew a short distance from the court. He knew that jurors, as a rule, wouldn't go there. He bought two pints and steak and kidney pies for them both.

'There's no more we can do now. It's in the lap of the Gods but I expect trouble with Parveen.'

———◆◆◆◆———

Chapter 27
The Trial Continued

The court re-assembled at 2:15 p.m. The courtroom was stuffy. The accused sat quietly in the dock. It was obvious that the two brothers were not talking to the three Sheffield defendants. Each sat with their eyes to the front, not communicating.

Turnbull thought how incongruous it looked. A modern court, yet people in wigs. They looked totally out of context.

Prosecuting counsel called his first witness, Parveen Ashkani. Parveen, wearing Asian clothing, walked into the court accompanied by a lady usher. Parveen looked around the court to see who was where. She saw her brothers in the dock and smiled at them as she took her place in the witness box.

Before the court clerk had an opportunity to ask the witness to take the oath, Parveen turned to the judge and said, 'I don't wish to give evidence.'

'I'm afraid you don't have a choice in the matter,' the judge said to her. 'You are a material witness and you are required to give evidence. Would you like some advice from a barrister who I can assign to you as to your position?'

'Yes, please,' she replied. She spoke clearly but softly and with confidence.

'Mr Beecroft, do you know whether counsel is available to advise this witness as to her rights?'

'Yes, Milord, we have asked Mr Green of counsel to stand by, lest he be required for this purpose.'

'Excellent, we'll adjourn for that to happen. Members of the jury, you have heard what is happening. We will adjourn for the witness to be advised. Please go to your jury room. There is time for you to have a coffee.'

'All rise,' ordered the court clerk. The judge and jury retired and the silence was broken by conversations between counsel and their solicitors. The ushers filled the jurors' water glasses and the one in the witness box.

Half an hour passed and court re-assembled.

'All stand,' said the court clerk as the judge returned to court.

'Yes, Mr Green?'

'Milord, I have advised Parveen Ashkani of her rights and she now agrees to give evidence. I have not discussed what she will say.'

'Thank you, let the witness be sworn.'

Parveen Ashkani then swore on the Koran to give evidence that would be the truth, the whole truth and nothing but the truth.

'May I call you Parveen?' asked Mr. Beecroft.

'Yes,' she confirmed.

'Is what you said to the police, in your witness statement and in interview, the truth?'

'Yes,' she replied.

'Did your brothers hit you?'

'No, they never have.'

'Then why say to the police that they hit you?'

'I don't know.'

'You said to the police that your brothers were to pay to have you and your husband killed. Was that true?'

'No.'

'Then why did you say that?'

'My brothers did not say this or anything like it. I don't know why I told this to the police. I was confused and upset.'

'Have you, before this trial, been living with your family, for example your brothers, father and mother?'

'Yes.'

'Your brothers, Nadeem and Wahid, have been in custody

since their arrest, awaiting trial. Have you been talking to your brother Nadeem and to your brother Wahid in prison by telephone?'

'Yes.'

'Have you been visiting them in prison?'

'Yes.'

'In your witness statement you told the police that these two brothers were responsible for hiring men to kill your husband.'

'Yes.'

'Why tell the police your brothers were responsible for your husband's death if that was not the case?'

'I was thinking, when I spoke to the police, that my brothers could be responsible. I told the police this so that they could help with my husband's murder.'

'And thereby arrest your brothers?'

'Yes.'

'Milord,' said Beecroft. 'I have an application to make which should be made in the absence of the jury.'

'Members of the jury,' said the judge. 'Matters of law are for me and matters of fact are for you. A matter of law has arisen which I must rule upon in your absence, so would you kindly retire to the jury room whilst I do that.'

'Thank you, Milord,' said Beecroft.

'Yes, Mr Beecroft,' said the judge, once the jury had retired.

'Milord, this witness made a statement, which is before you, stating in the clearest terms that her brothers commissioned three Sheffield men to murder her husband. She now wishes to go back on that statement and thereby demonstrates a hostile animus towards the party calling her, namely The Crown.

'Ordinarily, of course, we could not cross-examine the witness as we are calling her and she is our witness. But, in the circumstances, we apply for leave to treat her as a hostile witness and to cross-examine her upon her witness statement which she made voluntarily and signed for its accuracy.'

'Thank you, Mr Beecroft. Miss Davies, Mr Archbold, can you oppose this application?'

'No,' replied both counsel.

'I think that's very wise,' said the judge. 'Bring the jury back.'

Turnbull turned to Jasper. 'That's a surprise. The jury will now hear the whole of her witness statement. This is good, because the jury will think she told the truth in her statement and is now going back on it.'

The jurors shuffled back into court in the same order in which they had been sworn and the judge addressed them.

'Members of the jury, prosecuting counsel has applied to treat this witness as hostile to The Crown and to cross-examine her on the statement to the police. Ordinarily, the party calling a witness is not permitted to challenge that witness's testimony, but when the witness demonstrates hostility to the party calling her, in this case The Crown, that party can apply to cross-examine the witness on her witness statement on the grounds that she is a hostile witness.

'That is what has happened in your absence and I have granted the application.

'You will now hear Mr Beecroft cross-examine the witness upon her witness statement.

'Yes, Mr Beecroft.'

'Thank you, My Lord.'

'Had you, before returning to your family, been living with your husband's family in Halifax?'

'Yes, I wasn't telling a lie.'

'Let us see what is true in your statement and what is a lie.'

'Is it true, when in Halifax, days before the murder, you made your husband lie down in the car?'

'Yes.'

'Did you change the phone number for his home in Halifax?'

'Yes.'

'So both of those parts of your statement are true?'

'Yes.'

'Why change his number?'

'I took a call asking if Mahmood Asgar was there. I said, "This is the wrong number". I asked Mahmood "How does someone know your telephone number?" He said he didn't know.'

'Who did it sound like?'

'Mahmood said "It's not your brother, the man spoke differently".'

'Did it ring again?'

'Yes. The phone rang continuously up to eleven o'clock at night, but I didn't answer it.'

'How long did your husband live at 8 Grove Road?'

'A short time. A matter of weeks.'

'Were you living at your family home, also in Halifax?'

'Yes.'

'Did your mother know he was at Grove Road?'

'Yes, but she didn't tell my brothers. I was waiting for a right time to explain I was married, but there was never a right time. I was confused. I didn't know what to do.'

'Is it true you took Mahmood Asgar on the Sunday to a car boot sale and then to Cannon Mills?'

'Yes.'

'So that bit of your statement is right?'

'Yes.'

'And you took him food?'

'Yes.'

'So that's right?'

'Yes.'

'Did Nadeem say "I've had a dream"?'

'Yes, but the dream he said was that our mother had died.'

'That's not what you told the police.'

'I was confused.'

'Is it true you went back to his house after swimming?'

'Yes.'

'And he wasn't there?'

'No.'

'So that bit's right?'

'Yes.'

'When you got home that day, was your father singing "Today God has listened. What I wanted has happened today"?'

'Yes. The police were telling me my brothers had done it and I believed them, so went along with it.'

'There are things in the witness statement which are true but, equally, as we shall see, there are many which are not true. Were you deliberately lying?'

'No.'

Mr Beecroft then took the witness, at length, through the witness statement she had made, some of which she said was true and denying that those parts which implicated her brothers were true.

'I suggest, Parveen, that the whole of your witness statement is true. You deny only those parts which implicate your brothers in the murder. Is that not so?'

'No.'

'And you are now trying to find a way to get round what you said to the police?'

'No.'

'The truth is that your brothers did tell you they threatened to kill your husband.'

'No.'

'And when he was murdered, you assumed they were responsible?'

'No.'

'Can you think of anyone in the United Kingdom who would want your husband murdered?'

'No.'

'And now you find yourself torn between loyalty to your husband who is dead and to your brothers who are alive. He had, after all, only been here a short time and, on your own account, had hardly met anyone. Is that true?'

'Yes.'

'Thank you, Parveen,' said Tom Beecroft as he sat down.

'We'll adjourn now until tomorrow morning,' said the judge. 'In the meantime, members of the jury, please do not talk to anyone outside your own number. And, if you talk amongst yourselves, please do so in the privacy of your jury room.'

The jury withdrew.

'All rise,' said the clerk as the Judge shuffled out of court.

'He didn't make as much ground as we hoped,' said Turnbull to Jasper as they walked out of court.

'No,' said Jasper. 'Maybe he didn't want to seem a bully. Let's have a coffee in the police room.'

They went through the door marked "Police Only" and sat down. There were several other police officers there who were waiting to give evidence in other cases.

'Coffee, Dave?'

'Yes, please.'

'What did you think?'

'Well, her statement is now before the jury and her avoidance of the bits incriminating her brothers didn't sound at all convincing.'

'I agree,' said Turnbull. 'Tomorrow we will see whether the defence makes any ground.'

Chapter 28

The Trial Continued

The court re-assembled at 10:30 the following morning. The cross-examination of Parveen was eagerly awaited. The court hushed as the judge swept into court.

'Yes, Miss Davies?' said the judge. 'It's your turn to cross-examine Parveen on behalf of Nadeem Khan.'

'Thank you, Milord. Parveen, you made a witness statement blaming your brothers, Nadeem and Wahid, for the murder of your husband. Did anyone put you up to blaming them?'

'My in-laws. They said Nadeem and Wahid were responsible and so I said these things against them to get them into trouble. I exaggerated. I made things look bad. I added things. I regret telling those lies, but I am now telling the truth.' Parveen sobbed and looked at her brothers in the dock.

'May I go back to your first visit to Pakistan? Is it unusual for Pakistani children to be sent to Pakistan?'

'No.'

'Did you exaggerate when you said you didn't go to school for two years?'

'Yes, it was not true.'

'Were you able to contact your family when you were in Pakistan?'

'No.'

'Why?'

'There was no telephone in the house. The public phone booth was ten to fifteen minutes' drive away.'

'Were you and Nadeem taken to the public phone to speak to your family in the UK?'

'Yes.'

'Did you write home?'

'Yes, but I think Uncle Rashid was not posting the letters. In any case, my mother can't read or write, so she sent tapes for me to listen to what she wanted to say.'

'Did you receive those tapes?'

'Yes.'

'And did you listen to them?'

'Yes.'

'Without objection from the family?'

'Yes.'

'Nadeem went home in 1994, but you stayed. Why?'

'The elders in the community decided I should stay. I went home when I was fourteen or fifteen.'

'Why did you not want to marry your cousin?'

'He has mental problems. Too many cousins marry and that led to mental health problems from inter-breeding.' Those in the gallery murmured disapproval.

Turnbull thought that the politically correct would have a field day with that answer.

'When you were in the UK, did you have problems with Nadeem?'

'No, he was busy working and having a good time. He was seldom at home. He wasn't involved in my life at all. He wasn't interested in me.' Parveen again looked at her brothers and smiled.

'Where did you go after the murder?'

'The police did not want me to stay in the same house as my brothers. My in-laws had come over after the death, so I stayed with them in Hipperholme,'

'Who did they hold responsible for their son's death?'

'Nadeem and Wahid. They blamed them for the killing and Nadeem for the breakdown of his marriage to their daughter, Aisha.'

'What were they saying?'

'Nadeem had done it. They put things into my head. When I spoke to the police I tried to make it worse for Nadeem. In later interviews I was exaggerating wildly what had happened. I had several interviews, not just one.'

'What was Nadeem like to you in Pakistan?'

'He was nice.'

'Did you talk to him about personal matters?'

'No, he wasn't interested.'

'You spoke of a dream he said he had?'

'Yes.'

'Was his dream in any way threatening to Asgar?'

'No. I am still getting phone calls from Pakistan wanting justice for Asgar.'

'Do you believe now that Nadeem was involved in Asgar's death?'

'No.'

'You have another brother, do you not?'

'Yes, Abdul Mahmood. He is sixteen, nearly seventeen.'

'How do you get on with him?'

'Very well.'

'Where is he?'

'In Pakistan.'

'When did he go?'

'The day you say my husband was murdered.'

'Why did he go?'

'I don't know.'

'How did a sixteen-year-old boy just up and fly to Pakistan? The family must have arranged it for him and got him a passport, given him money, arranged for somewhere for him to stay.'

'If my parents did it, I was not aware of it.'

'Did you say goodbye?'

'No.'

'So he just disappeared?'

'Yes.'

'You're lying.'

'No.'

'Are the family in touch with him?'

'No.'

'Why not?'

'We don't know where he is.'

'But he's only sixteen. Aren't you worried?'

'No.'

'Did he have any malice towards your husband?'

'I don't know. One day he saw me with injuries to my face.'

'Did he ask you how you got them?'

'Yes.'

'Did he know you were married?'

'Yes.'

'And that your husband was in the UK?'

'Yes.'

'Who caused the injuries?'

'I don't want to say.'

'Why not?'

'I'm just not saying.'

'No further questions.'

'Now, Mr Archbold, your turn on behalf of Wahid,' said the judge.

'Thank you, Milord. How did you feel about Asgar's family after his death?'

'I felt I owed a duty to them. They were blaming my family when I was living with them. There was pressure to tell the police things which weren't true.'

'Has Wahid ever been violent to you?'

'No.'

'Why were you sent to Pakistan with Wahid?'

'Because Wahid and I had been troublesome and disobedient at home.'

'Who made the decision that you should return to the UK?'

'I did. I told Uncle Rashid that my parents knew I was
returning, which was a lie.'

'On arrival in the UK, did you get in touch with the police?'

'Yes.'

'Had that anything to do with the problems with Wahid?'

'No.'

'Did Wahid cause you problems?'

'No, I had no problems with Wahid.'

'Did he ever break your mobile phone?'

'Yes, because he and Nadeem suspected I was talking to
someone they did not know about. Rumours were spreading in
Pakistan that I'd got engaged.'

'Why tell the police Wahid had hit you?'

'I said to the police that Wahid had hit me because my
mother-in-law told me to say that. I added Nadeem had as well
to make it look bad for them. My husband told me Wahid had
telephoned him and threatened to kill him, but Wahid himself
never said that.'

'Why did you leave home to go to Cardiff?'

'Because Mum and Dad argued all the time. Narinda said
she would help me and I thought of going to Cardiff. Then I was
going to bring Asgar over to the UK.'

'Did your husband have a leisure card?'

'Yes. It was a joint card, in both our names, that we used
for the library and to go swimming and for a sauna. We tried to
have some sort of life together, but it was very difficult.'

'Was he a prisoner in his own home?'

'No, he wasn't a prisoner in his home, but he never went
out except with me occasionally. No one visited him as far as I
know. He couldn't speak English. He only had the money I got

for him. I felt so sorry for him, but at least we had some time together.'

Parveen sobbed and blew her nose into the tissue which the usher passed to her.

'Have you been in contact with the police family liaison officers?'

'Yes, they wanted to keep me away from my brothers, but I insisted I wanted to go back to live with them.'

'Were you frightened of your brothers?'

'No. I hardly ever saw them. We all lived our own lives.'

'Was Nadeem arrested?'

'Yes.'

'Was he in custody after that?'

'Yes.'

'Did you visit him in prison?'

'Yes, many times.'

'When did you return to Pakistan?'

'In October 2004 to get married. The marriage certificate was back-dated to 2002 to help Asgar get his visa. That was his idea, not mine.'

'Did Wahid ever strike you with a stick and chase you?'

'No. I had a stick, not him.'

'Did either brother say they were going to kill you?'

'No, they never said they were going to kill us. Nor did they say it would cost three or four thousand. It's all lies.'

'When did you return to the UK?'

'November 2004. Wahid came to collect me from the airport. He was pleased to see me. I didn't tell him I had just got married.'

'You have another younger brother, as you have told us?'

'Yes, Abdul Mahmood.'

'Does Abdul have a telephone?'

'Yes he has. We used to borrow each other's phones and

SIM cards which were in credit. I would use other people's phones to call my husband.'

'We are, in due course, to hear from Saber Malik in Cardiff and I wanted to ask you whether you said to him various things about yourself and your brothers?'

'Yes.'

'Did you tell him about your older brothers being violent to you?'

'No.'

'Did you tell him you were frightened of your brothers?'

'No.'

'Did you ever tell him you were married to someone in Pakistan?'

'No.'

'Did you say your in-laws knew you were married?'

'No.'

'Did you tell him you were scared of your brothers?'

'No.'

'Did you say if they caught you they would kill you?'

'No.'

'This man befriended you?'

'Yes.'

'Why should he lie about you?'

'I don't know.'

'Did you sign every page of your witness statement to say it was true?'

'Yes.'

'Why have you said all these things against your two eldest brothers?'

'Because my in-laws said so.'

'You are alleged to have said things to Narinda and to the police liaison officers. You know them?'

'Yes.'

'Did you say any of these things to them?'

'No.'

'Are you just being loyal to your brothers?'

'No.'

'Did you speak to Wahid by telephone when he was in custody?'

'Yes, but I didn't say anything to incriminate them.'

'No further questions.'

'Any questions on behalf of Omar Fazal, Mr Archbold?'

'One question, if I may, Milord,' said Mr Archbold as he turned to address Parveen.

'Do you know Fazal?'

'No.'

'Thank you, no more questions.'

'Any questions, Mr May?' asked the judge.

'No questions on behalf of Sam Leonard.'

'Any questions on behalf of Rastrick?'

'No, Milord,' said Mr Mountfield.

'Any re-examination, Mr Beecroft?'

'Yes, My Lord.'

'Parveen, may I understand the reason for the blame you attached to your elder brothers, Nadeem and Wahid, in the witness statement you made to the police on the day following your husband's murder? You say you blamed them because your in-laws persuaded you that they were to blame.'

'Yes, sir.'

'But you made your statement immediately upon being brought to Bradford from Halifax and just after you had discovered Asgar was not at 8 Grove Road?'

'Yes.'

'So you had no opportunity to speak to your in-laws until after you had made your witness statement?'

'No.'

'You went to live with them *after* you had made your witness statement did you not?'

'Yes.'

'So they came to the UK after the murder and not before?'

'Yes.'

'So they cannot have had any effect on what you said in your statement?'

'No, they did. The statement took several days to do and, in Pakistan, they said to me that if anything happened to me, my elder brothers would be to blame.'

'Any other reason?'

'Yes, when the tape wasn't switched on, the police kept saying to me that my brothers were responsible. I was very upset. Surely if there was an honour killing, they would have killed me as well wouldn't they?'

'No more questions, Parveen.'

The witness retired.

'Now, Mr Beecroft, what comes next?' asked the judge.

'Milord, we now have a succession of witnesses, to whom reference has just been made, of what Parveen said to them about her brothers' behaviour. Mr Oldroyd will take those witnesses.'

'Thank you. Yes, Mr Oldroyd?'

Mr Oldroyd, junior counsel for the Crown, arose from his seat behind Mr Beecroft.

'I call Narinda,' said Mr Oldroyd 'This witness wishes to give evidence under this pseudonym to avoid disclosure of true identity. Any objections from counsel?'

'No,' replied each in turn.

An elegant, Asian woman in her fifties, walked into court. Her hair was tied back in a bun. She wore a smart, dark suit and high-heel shoes. She had an aura of professionalism, yet kindness, about her.

The witness then took the oath.

'Do you go by the pseudonym Narinda?'

'Yes, I do.'

'Will you write out your true name on this piece of paper and pass it to My Lord.'

'Yes.' Narinda wrote her true name on the paper and passed it to the judge who wrote it in his notebook and passed the paper to the clerk on his left who, in turn, passed it to the court clerk sitting before the judge.

'Are you a professional counsellor?' asked Mr Oldroyd.

'Yes, I am.'

'Do you work for the Calderdale Women's Centre in Halifax?'

'Yes, I do.'

She then gave evidence of what Parveen had said to her about her brothers' cruelty. She agreed with defence counsel that she relied wholly on what Parveen told her and never saw a mark on her.

'Next, Milord, I call Saber Malik,' said Mr Oldroyd.

Into the court walked a young Asian man who looked barely old enough to have left school. He looked lost and apprehensive. He took the oath on the Koran, in English, which he spoke with an Asian accent.

'Is your name Saber Malik?'

'Yes, please.'

'In September 2003, did Parveen Ashkani come to live at your house?'

'Yes, please.'

'In what circumstances?'

'I took pity on her, you know what I mean, because she was living in a hotel. I said she could come and live at my house, which she did. My mother agreed.'

'How long did she stay?'

'Two months.'

'Did she confide in you?'

'Yes, please.'

'Saying what?'

'She said there were family problems. They wouldn't let her do what she wanted and wouldn't let her out of the house. They beat her.'

'No more questions.'

'Any questions, Miss Davies?'

'Yes, Milord. Is your witness statement the truth?'

'Yes.'

'In that you say there were threats to beat her, but not that she had been beaten. Why the difference?'

'I don't know why I said that. She said she was scared and that if her brothers caught her, they would kill her. She was sad inside.'

'She said nothing about threats to kill her husband?'

'Not that I remember.'

'You are then totally reliant on her word?'

'Yes.'

'You never heard any threats?'

'No, but they came to get her. She did not want to go. She was trying to hide. About two hours later, I saw them driving past the house. They were pointing at it.'

'Thank you.'

'Any more questions?' asked the judge.

'No, Milord,' said counsel in turn.

'Next, Milord, we call the father-in-law of Parveen, Tariq Khan. This witness is anxious to give his evidence today so he can return to Pakistan. He speaks fluent English.'

'I understand,' said the judge. 'Make this your last witness for today.'

'Very well, Milord.'

Tariq Khan walked into court. A distinguished looking, middle-aged man, very smartly dressed and with his grey hair swept back from his face.

Turnbull thought he looked like Imran Khan, the celebrated Pakistan cricket captain who married Jemima Goldsmith.

'Is your name Tariq Khan?'

'Yes.'

'What is your occupation?'

'I'm a Member of Parliament in Pakistan.'

'Was your son Mahmood Asgar?'

'Yes.'

'We know he was killed on the sixth of February, 2005. Is Parveen Ashkani your daughter-in-law?'

'Yes.'

'How did you and she get on?'

'Very well. I viewed her as my daughter. She had married my son.'

'When they were married, did they live in a house owned by you in Dinga?'

'Yes.'

'Did Parveen then return to the UK?'

'Yes, leaving her husband in Pakistan.'

'She returned, she has told us, to the family home in Parkinson Lane, Halifax. Is that right?'

'Yes.'

'Did your son then come to the UK?'

'Yes.'

'Were you happy about that?'

'No.'

'Did he live at his uncle's house in Oldham before moving to Halifax?'

'Yes.'

'Did you speak to him by telephone?'

'Yes.'

'What was his attitude towards moving to Halifax?'

'He was frightened.'

'We know your daughter, Aisha, married Nadeem Khan, Parveen's brother.'

'Yes.'

'So two of your children married into the same family?'

'Yes.'

'Did that marriage break up?'

'Yes.'

'Did you know what Parveen's brothers' attitude was towards Asgar's marriage to their sister?'

'Yes, they were very much against it, for reasons I could never understand. He was a lovely, bright boy, and Parveen and he were very much in love.'

'Did you know what your son's intention was?'

'Yes, he wanted to return to Pakistan in March, 2005.'

'Did he say why?'

'Yes, because he'd been receiving threatening phone calls. Other times, when the telephone rang and he picked it up, no one would answer. I didn't want Parveen and Mahmood to marry. We were scared for them. I didn't like Nadeem. We're an educated family and Parveen's family are ignorant people.'

'After your son's death, did Parveen come to live with you in the UK?'

'Yes, we'd come over for my son's funeral. We were staying with friends in Hipperholme.'

'Did you, at any time, try to influence her in what she said in her witness statement?'

'No, I didn't even see her until after she'd made her witness statement. It was the idea of the police that she should come to stay with us.'

'At any time before she made her witness statement, did you

try to turn her mind against her brothers?'

'No, we wanted the best for them both, and although we had reservations about the marriage and her brothers, we did not speak of them.'

'Did the fact of the marriage cause you upset?'

'Yes.'

'Were you aware of any threats to your son?'

'Yes, he spoke to us on the telephone from England in late January, 2005.'

'Did you speak to Parveen about these threats?'

'She told us about threats to her life when she lived in Pakistan with my son. That was why she returned to the UK. But we never put any pressure on her as to what she should say.'

'Thank you.'

'Any counsel wish to cross-examine?' asked the judge.

'Yes, Milord,' said Miss Davies on behalf of Nadeem. 'Did you ever hear Nadeem making any threats?'

'No.'

'So you are reliant on what your son and your daughter-in-law said to you for your account?'

'Yes.'

'Did there come a time when you disapproved of the marriage?'

'Yes.'

'And did you speak to Parveen about that?'

'No.'

'No more questions.'

'Any other counsel wish to cross-examine?' asked the judge.

'No, My Lord,' replied counsel in turn.

'That is the close of today's proceedings,' said the judge. 'Remember my warnings, members of the jury – no talking.'

The members of the jury filed out of court.

'All rise,' said the court clerk and the judge left the court.

Turnbull and Jasper left court. They had managed to get a parking space in a car park opposite, so were able to get out of Sheffield before rush hour.

'What do you think?' asked Turnbull.

'Well,' said Jasper, 'I thought Tariq Khan was an impressive witness. Measured and clear in what he said. The idea of him putting Parveen up to making false allegations against her brothers just doesn't add up. We kept her close, when she came from Halifax, to protect ourselves against precisely this suggestion.'

'Well, the defence have to think of some explanation as to why he implicated her brothers and this is their only route.'

'I suppose so,' said Jasper.

The next morning, court re-assembled at 10:35. Both counsel were late and the judge looked displeased.

'Now, Mr Beecroft,' said the judge, 'there are some admissions I believe.'

'Yes, Milord,' said Beecroft.

The judge addressed the jury. 'One way of adducing evidence is by written admissions, signed by counsel, for all parties. It saves reading out volumes of witness statements. It is admitted by all counsel that on the tenth of November, 2004, Wahid was sentenced to three-and-a-half years' imprisonment and that he shared a cell with Asif Khan who, on the fourth of August, 2004, was sentenced to six-and-a-half years' imprisonment for an offence of blackmail.

'The Crown admits that the circumstances of his offence were that he exploited the family of a missing man by extorting money from them.'

Turnbull and Jasper anxiously awaited the evidence of Asif Khan. His evidence was crucial in the case against Wahid.

'Our next witness, Milord, is Asif Khan,' said Mr Beecroft.

Asif was brought into court by two prison officers. He was handcuffed to one of them. He looked scruffy and unshaven. *Not a good start,* thought Turnbull.

Asif did not need an interpreter. He took the oath on the Koran.

Beecroft addressed Asif.

'Is your name Asif Khan?'

'Yes.'

'Are you a prisoner in Leeds Prison?'

'Yes.'

'Are you serving a sentence of six years, six months?'

'Yes.'

'Mr Khan, did you share a cell with Wahid Mahmood between the fifth of January, 2005 and the twentieth of January, 2005?' asked Mr Beecroft.

'Yes.'

'Were mobile phones allowed?'

'No, but they were easy to get. A visitor brought me one in.'

'Did Wahid use your mobile?'

'Yes, we shared it.'

'Whom did he phone?'

'His brother, Nadeem, and his youngest brother, Abdul, amongst others.'

'Did Wahid speak to you about these calls?'

'Yes, he was depressed and fed up. He said someone was messing with his sister. He didn't say who. I heard him say to his brother "We should get rid of him".'

'What else did he say?'

'He mentioned a job that would cost five to eight thousand and he said something about Sheffield. He said the job could be done in two weeks and if he'd been out of prison, he'd have got the job done himself. He said two white guys and one black guy would do the job.'

'What happened to the phone?'

'The one I told you about before was confiscated, so I got another, and then that was confiscated.'

'Did you have a television set in the community area?'

'Yes. I saw reports on TV about a murder.'

'Did Wahid say anything to you about it?'

'Yes, we were in a queue for our dinner and he said "He's been taken care of, the job has been done, she brought shame on our family". He said "We should have taken care of our sister too".'

'Did he speak to you about it again?'

'Yes, a few days later he said that his sister was married to the dead man and that his brother, Nadeem, had been arrested.'

'Did you ever speak to Nadeem direct?'

'Yes, Wahid asked me to ring him. Nadeem said that if the police came to see Wahid to say he's only been to Cardiff once to pick up his mum.'

'When did you stop sharing a cell?'

'The end of January, 2005, but I continued to lend him my phone.'

'Did you ever speak to his younger brother, Abdul Mahmood?'

'Yes, Wahid asked me to ring him to find out what was happening at the house.'

'Have you made these things up for your own purposes?'

'No.'

'Why did he trust you?'

'Because we shared a cell and he asked me to make calls to each brother. We knew each other from outside.'

'Has anyone offered you money?'

'Yes. I got a call from someone offering me seventy thousand not to give evidence. He was Asian and spoke partly in Punjabi. I said I would do so to keep people off my back, but

I never heard from him again. It was not me making the offer, it was the Asian man. I was not blackmailing the family for seventy thousand.'

'That is all the questions I have,' said Beecroft.

'Mr Archbold, you represent Wahid, the man with whom the witness shared a cell, do you wish to cross-examine?' asked the judge.

'Yes, My Lord.'

'The offence of blackmail, for which you are serving six years' imprisonment, were you the prime mover?'

'No.'

'The sentencing judge, in his sentencing remarks, said he was satisfied you were the prime mover.'

'Yes.'

'So he got it wrong?'

'Yes.'

'And you received £14,000 from the victims of the blackmail?'

'Yes.'

'Which you were meant to share with your fellow blackmailers?'

'Yes.'

'But you didn't?'

'No.'

'So you swindled them as well?'

'Yes.'

'And you did not plead guilty to blackmail until the very last moment, the first day of your trial?'

'Yes.'

'And you hoped that by offering to give evidence against your fellow blackmailers that you would receive a lesser sentence?'

'Yes.'

'You were offered, and indeed accepted the offer, of seventy thousand to withdraw your witness statement in this case?'

'Yes, to keep them off my back. The man made threats that if I didn't accept, my family would suffer.'

'You were the one who rang a number you were given in order to obtain the seventy thousand by threats?'

'No, he rang me.'

Were you, as a result of agreeing to give evidence for the Crown, transferred from Leeds Prison to Kirklevington Prison?'

'Yes.'

'Is that a less restricted regime?'

'Yes.'

'So you derived a benefit from telling the police about Wahid?'

'Yes.'

'Whilst at Kirklevington, did you report a man for writing graffiti on a prison wall?'

'Yes.'

'Were you then segregated from the other prisoners?'

'Yes.'

'That was a benefit?'

'Yes.'

'It was all lies, wasn't it? You wanted to ingratiate yourself with the governor?'

'No.'

'The reason you have given evidence against Wahid is to gain a benefit for yourself?'

'No. I have come forward because it was the right thing to do.'

'In your defence statement, setting out your defence to the blackmail offence, in advance of the trial, before you pleaded guilty, did you allege that the family had made up the allegations?'

'Yes.'

'You said it was an elaborate trick by the victim's family?'

'Yes.'

'That was a complete lie?'

'Yes.'

'Did you believe that if you gave a statement against Wahid, you would get a reduced sentence?'

'Yes.'

'And you did the same in relation to your blackmail offence?'

'Yes.'

'And were you, as a result of making the statement against Wahid, not only moved to a new prison, but your category was reduced from C to D?'

'Yes.'

'The conditions were now more pleasant?'

'Yes.'

'And there were more work opportunities?'

'Yes.'

'Were you also closer, in distance, to your family?'

'Yes.'

'The truth is that Wahid never spoke to you about Asgar's murder. You have made it all up to gain advantage for yourself.'

'No.'

'Thank you.'

'Mr Beecroft,' asked the judge, 'have you questions in re-examination?'

'Yes, Milord,' replied Mr Beecroft. He turned to the witness box.

'How has giving evidence affected you?'

'My life has been made hell. My family and I have been repeatedly threatened.'

'Why did you go ahead?'

'Because it is the right thing to do.'

'Thank you, Mr. Khan.'

'We will adjourn there until tomorrow,' said the judge. 'Remember my warnings, members of the jury.'

The following morning, Turnbull and Jasper resigned themselves to a dull day in court when the prosecution tied up the loose ends of their case.

This was done mostly by the reading of statements which were not in dispute, and the handing out, to the jury, of written admissions of salient facts which had been culled from other statements not in dispute.

Turnbull was surprised to discover there were no questions from the defence teams as to the DNA evidence of Leonard's secretion on the cigarette tab recovered from the scene. Turnbull wondered where the investigation would have got without that breakthrough.

Evidence was then read out that Leonard and Fazal were not at work on the night of the eleventh of February.

Joe Ogden's statement was read about the purchase of the car and the tracing of Rastrick's telephone number.

The prosecution then called evidence that at 7:46 p.m. on the sixth of February, a vehicle corresponding to the Ogden's car was caught on CCTV near to the deceased's address. The car was a Rover 400 manufactured between 1990 and 1995, with a sunroof, just like Ogden's car. Also, a Rover could easily be mistaken for a Peugeot, or vice versa.

The expert called stated that both cars, the Rover and the Peugeot, were three-box mid-sized saloons with a similar profile.

The two Sheffield officers gave evidence that Mr Ogden's car was intact, near to Tinsley Golf Club, at 11:40 a.m. on sixth February and burnt out by 10:08 p.m.: that Fazal and Leonard arrived at the Rose and Crown in a Rover car and they left at 10:22 p.m.

The members of the jury were shown the video of the two

men in the Rose and Crown public house.

The Crown then called Fazal's girlfriend, Sandra Jaimes, as to what he said to her about setting up a false alibi; that he said he was the driver on the night and the man taken from the house was shot, he didn't say by whom.

When cross-examined by Fazal's counsel, she agreed he had never treated her badly or been violent to her, that she was now a protected witness and the police paid for her rent.

She agreed that she had lied in her first witness statement, falsely giving him an alibi, and that before she made her second witness statement, which contained the truth, she had been arrested for attempting to pervert the course of justice by giving him a false alibi. However, she stuck to her account that Fazal had asked her to give a false alibi for the sixth of February before the sixth of February, not after.

Next, the Crown called Helen Munro, Rastrick's girlfriend. She saw Rastrick when he was in prison, on the eleventh of March, awaiting trial for a second shooting later in February 2005, to which he pleaded guilty. His telephone numbers ended in 177 and 222. He told her that he went in a car when a man was collected, taken to the moor and shot. You will remember their conversation was bugged.

The Crown called evidence about the circumstances of the second shooting and Rastrick's possession of the gun used.

A telephone schedule was produced showing contact between the various phones attributed to the defendants and contact between Nadeem and Wahid with the deceased's home.

Cell site evidence was called as to the area in which the calls were made.

Finally, the Crown called evidence as to arrests and inter-views of the five accused.

'That, Milord, is the case for the prosecution,' said Mr Beecroft.

Chapter 29
The Trial Continued

Turnbull and Jasper went out for lunch to a little Italian restaurant Turnbull knew. The proprietor greeted him and took them to a table by the window, looking out on to a pedestrian precinct. Both ordered linguine vongole and a glass of Pinot Grigio.

'What do you think?' asked Turnbull.

'Well,' said Jasper, 'it will be interesting to see who of the defendants gives evidence. I think it's pretty nailed on except for the case against Wahid. Asif Khan's evidence was not as strong as we'd hoped.'

'I agree, he wasn't very strong,' said Turnbull.

The court reassembled at 2:15 p.m. and all present waited with baited breath to see which of the defendants, if any, would give evidence.

Counsel for Nadeem, Miss Davies Q.C., stood. 'I call Nadeem Khan.'

Nadeem moved from the dock into the witness box, accompanied by a prison officer. He took the oath on the Koran. He was smartly dressed in a suit and tie.

'Are you Nadeem Khan?'

'Yes.'

'Were you born in Pakistan?'

'Yes.'

'When did you come to the UK?'

'1981.'

'Where did you live?'

'With my family at 16 Parkinson Lane.'

'Your family being?'

'My mum and dad, my brothers Wahid Mahmood and Abdul

Mahmood and my sister Parveen Ashkani.'

'Did you return to Pakistan?'

'Yes, in 1987 and I stayed there until 1994 when I returned to England.'

'Where did you go to school?'

'I went to local schools, which I left when I was sixteen with three GCSEs, and then I went to Calderdale College to do business studies. After that I went to Huddersfield Tech to do a diploma.'

'What did you do then?'

'I bought and sold cars.'

'When did you start your restaurant?'

'In 2002.'

'How is that going?'

'Well, I work long hours. I spend little time at home. When I'm not working, I spend my time with my girlfriend. I'm seldom at home. You're only on this earth once.'

'How much do you earn?'

'About twelve thousand a year.'

Oh yes, thought Turnbull, *how was the Porsche paid for?*

'Tell me about Parveen. Were you in Pakistan when she came out with her mother and Wahid?'

'Yes.'

'How was she?'

'Happy. I never saw her mistreated.'

'Have you ever been violent to her?'

'No.'

'Could she ring home?'

'Yes, from a telephone box not far away.'

'When did you return to the UK?'

'1994. Parveen remained in Pakistan.'

'When did she return?'

'1997. We went to college together.'

'Did she return to Pakistan?'

'Yes, in 2002, with me and Wahid for a holiday.'

'Were any restrictions imposed upon her?'

'I'd drive her into town and she was free to do what she wanted within reason.'

'You married in 2002?'

'Yes, I married Aisha Khan. Her brother was Mahmood Asgar. They were from a good family.'

'When did you return to the UK?'

'In November 2002 with Wahid. Parveen returned in December 2002 and she came to Parkinson Lane.'

'Did you see her at home?'

'Yes, weekly. She got on fine with everyone. There were no problems.'

'Why should she say to the police that she was being mistreated?'

'I have no idea.'

'Who was Parveen expected to marry?'

'Well, not Rashid's son as there is mental illness in the family.'

'Did you know Parveen married Aisha's brother secretly?'

'No.'

'We know Parveen left home and went to Cardiff.'

'Yes, I didn't know what was going on. I'm never home. I have my own life to lead.'

'Did you go to Cardiff?'

'Yes, with others, as Parveen had a lot of luggage.'

'Did you go to Saber Malik's house?'

'Yes.'

'Did she return home?'

'Yes.'

'Did you know that, in December 2004, Asgar came to the UK?'

'No.'

'Did you know they were married?'

'No. By now I was separated and divorced from Aisha.'

'Would you have objected to their marriage?'

'No.'

'What mobile phone did you have?'

'One with 033 numbers. I gave it to my younger brother, Abdul, once when I went abroad. He also borrowed it frequently when I was at home.'

'Can I turn to the weekend of the sixth of February, 2005? Where were you?'

'I went out to a nightclub and got home about 3:00 a.m. I slept 'til noon and then I went to the restaurant and got home about 10:30 p.m. I met my current girlfriend after work.'

'Was your father singing?'

'No.'

'Did you know that Asgar had been shot at 8:00 p.m.?'

'No.'

'What did you do on the sixth?'

'On the sixth I went to Leeds. After that I went home to find the police there. My family had been arrested.'

'When did you find out Asgar had been murdered?'

'On the seventh. I didn't even know he was in the UK then.'

'When were you arrested?'

'I was arrested and was interviewed on the eighth of February. I told the truth. I knew nothing about any murder. I was released on bail and went home. The family had also been released.'

'Have you ever tried to influence Parveen as to what she should say in this trial?'

'No. At the beginning, I was advised by my lawyer not to talk to her, but she returned to live at the family home. It was impossible not to talk with her. Our relationship was fine. I have never spoken to her about the case.'

Turnbull whispered to Jasper, 'The jury will never believe that.'

'Were you re-arrested?'

'Yes.'

'Did you speak to your younger brother, Abdul, about the arrests?'

'Yes, he was upset and panicky. He told me he knew Omar Fazal from clubbing. He got drugs from him. He used to ring him for coke and skunk. He said he felt he was to blame. He wanted to scare Asgar off from associating with our sister and so he got in touch with Fazal who said it would cost four to £500 to scare him off by roughing him up.

'I said "Why didn't you tell me what you were thinking and doing?" and he said he thought I wouldn't be interested or wouldn't believe him. He was only sixteen at the time.'

'Did you ask him why he wanted to scare him?'

'Yes. He said one day Parveen's face was red. It looked like someone had hit her, but when he asked her about it, she denied she had been hit. So he told Fazal to send someone to scare Asgar off as he knew it would be him. She had told Abdul she was seeing Asgar, but asked Abdul not to tell his brothers. I said that he must tell the police.'

'Did you tell the police?'

'No. I was scared to get Abdul into trouble. He said he would tell them about getting Fazal to scare him off.'

'Did you telephone your brother Wahid in prison?'

'Yes.'

'Was it to do with Asgar?'

'No.'

'Did you know when Abdul was using your phone?'

'Yes.'

'I left my phone at home when I was abroad coz calls from

abroad are very expensive. I was away between the twenty-second of January and the fifth of February.'

'Did you call Asgar?'

'No. I didn't know he was in the UK. Any calls to Fazal must have been made by Abdul.'

'Did you know Wahid shared a cell with Asif?'

'Yes. I didn't know him but I'd seen him around Halifax.'

'Did you discuss with Wahid a plan to harm Asgar?'

'No.'

'Was Sheffield discussed and a cost of five to £8,000?'

'No.'

'On the ninth of February, did you say to Wahid that Parveen should have been taken care of?'

'No.'

'Do you know any of the Sheffield defendants?'

'No.'

'Did you ever see Fazal in custody at Armley?'

'Yes. I was told he was in the same prison. He said he knew nothing about Asgar's murder. I asked him why he had been charged. He said his girlfriend had made a statement against him.

'I asked him whether he knew Abdul. He said "no" and walked off. Later, I asked him how it was that Abdul had his two telephone numbers stored on his phone. He said "Well, I do know Abdul."

'I asked him whether he had telephoned Asgar. He said that Leonard had used his phone and maybe Leonard had phoned, because he himself had never telephoned Asgar. I left it at that.'

'Did you ever speak to Sam Leonard?'

'Yes, one week before the trial began when I told him I knew everything, which was a lie, but I wanted him to tell the truth. He just said that he couldn't say anything. I asked him if he had used Fazal's phone. He said he didn't know how to use a phone.

'So I spoke to Fazal again and told him what Sam had said. He said that Jack Rastrick and Sam Leonard had been to Halifax to scare off Asgar. He wasn't saying anything else. He was scared of Jack Rastrick.'

'Did you speak to Sam Leonard again?'

'Yes. He said he was the driver. Rastrick got the man out of the house. He then asked Rastrick what he was doing. Sam said he wanted to know where to go and where to drop the man off. He had no idea he was going to be shot. He just thought he was to be scared off. Rastrick told him to just keep driving.

'Sam told me that as far as he knew, Rastrick was going to slap him up, but Rastrick got him out of the car, took him round the back and shot him. He then got back in the car and Sam asked him why he had done that. Rastrick replied "He could find out who I was. You told him we're from Sheffield. Get rid of the car and keep your mouth shut".

'So I spoke to Jack Rastrick and asked him his version. I asked him where his gun was and he said "Do you want me to put it in your garden? Keep your mouth shut". He kept saying that to Sam and Fazal, but I want to tell the truth. I had nothing to do with any attack or plan to scare Asgar off. I have never threatened to cause him harm.'

The judge said, 'This is a convenient moment for us to adjourn for lunch.'

Turnbull and Jasper went to the usual pub for sandwiches and a drink.

Turnbull said, "Now we know for the first time what Nadeem's defence is. He had nothing to do with Asgar's killing. His sixteen-year-old younger brother, Abdul, recruited Fazal, who was his drug supplier, to scare Asgar off because he had seen that his sister had been struck by him. The plan was to slap him up, but it went further because Sam Leonard blurted out, to the three in the car, that they were from Sheffield. Rastrick went beyond what the three had agreed. So Nadeem is placing the blame on Abdul and Jack Rastrick.

'That's why Abdul has gone to Pakistan where, surprise surprise, we can't trace him.'

After lunch, Nadeem was cross-examined by counsel for his brother, Wahid, who established that Abdul was sixteen in February, 2005, but looked much older.

When cross-examined on behalf of Rastrick, Nadeem said Rastrick had said to him, at reception in the prison, "If you go in the box and say anything, I'll kill your family".

Cross-examined by the prosecution, Nadeem was asked 'Why didn't you say before that Abdul was responsible?'

'It's only recently I've decided to tell the truth.'

'Did you mention any of this in your defence statement, put in before this trial, as to what your defence in this trial is?'

'No, I wanted to keep Abdul out of it.'

'There is no mention of Abdul being responsible for this death in your defence statement. Are you just trying to pass the buck to Rastrick because you know he's in custody for a second shooting?'

'No. I didn't want to grass on my sixteen-year-old brother.'

'Has Abdul been sent abroad so that he can be used as a scapegoat?'

'No.'

'Where is he?'

'I don't know.'

'Where was a sixteen-year-old going to get £500?'

'He worked as a packer and saved the money.'

'Did you not have any savings?'

'No.'

'What would you have thought if Parveen had married Asgar?'

'I would be happy.'

'Why did she then not want to tell you of her marriage?'

'I don't know. We weren't that close. None of what she has said about my violence is true. I have never threatened her or Asgar. All the calls on my phone, after my return from abroad, were from Abdul, not me.'

'Did you store Omar Fazal's number on your phone?'

'No.'

'Why not mention Abdul's part in the death when inter-viewed by the police?'

'Because he said he was handing himself in. If I'd told the police, I would have been thought of as a grass.'

'No more questions,' said Beecroft.

'Any re-examination, Miss Davies?' asked the judge.

'No, Milord.'

Chapter 30
The Trial Continues

'Now, Mr Archbold,' said the judge, 'it's your turn to present the case on behalf of Wahid.'

Those in court waited in anticipation to see if Wahid would give evidence, as his brother had done.

'Milord, yes, I call Wahid Mahmood to give evidence.'

Wahid Mahmood was escorted to the witness box and was sworn in. He looked anxiously at his brother in the dock.

'Are you Wahid Mahmood?'

'Yes.'

'Are you Nadeem's brother?'

'Yes.'

'Did you and he conscript another to murder Asgar?'

'No.'

'You are also Parveen's brother?'

'Yes.'

'What is your relationship with her like?'

'We have a good relationship.'

'In 2002 did you go with Nadeem and Parveen to Pakistan?'

'Yes, for what I thought was a two-week holiday. I came home in November and Parveen in December. I didn't know whilst there that she had got engaged. She returned home and everything was fine.'

'We know your brother and Aisha were divorced.'

'Yes.'

'Did Parveen leave home?'

'Yes, I didn't know why.'

'Did you ever go to Cardiff?'

'Yes, because Mum said to pick Parveen up. When I got

there, I didn't see Parveen. Then Nadeem arrived and then the police. We came home without Parveen.'

'Did she eventually return?'

'Yes, she rang me. I went to collect her. She said she'd been in Pakistan and got married. I asked her who she'd got married to. She told me, but I promised not to tell anyone. At home, the marriage was not revealed and Dad still talked of her marrying her cousin. She said she wasn't ready.'

'Were you sent to prison in November, 2004?'

'Yes for three and a half years for selling drugs.'

'Were you aware of any plan to kill Asgar and/or Parveen?'

'No. I wasn't even aware Asgar was in the country.'

'In November, were you in Armley gaol?'

'Yes.'

'And did you, for a time, share a cell with Asif Khan?'

'Yes. He also was from Halifax. I knew, because of his reputation, to be wary of him.'

'Did he have a mobile?'

'Yes. He said I could use it. So I used it to ring my family on it.'

'What happened to the phone?'

'It was seized in Armley gaol and I took the blame. He got a second phone with two SIM cards and I used them to ring my family.'

'Were you transferred out of the joint cell?'

'Yes.'

'Did you confide in Asif?'

'No.'

'When you rang home, did you talk about Parveen and her husband?'

'No, never in Asif's presence.'

'Did you ever say, "Someone's messing with my sister, we must get rid of him."?'

'No. I didn't discuss anything about my sister.'

'Did you say you'd agreed a plan with Nadeem to pay for the murder?'

'No. I am not a murderer.'

'When were you first aware of the murder?'

'On the TV. I rang home and was told by my uncle that the family had been arrested.'

'Did you say to Asif "The job's been done"?'

'No.'

'Did you become aware that Parveen had made a statement against you?'

'Yes. I wanted to know why she had lied. I was fuming.'

'Thank you, Wahid.'

'Miss Davies, have you any questions on behalf of Nadeem?' asked the judge.

'Yes, Milord.'

'Wahid, did you ever tell Nadeem that Parveen had married?'

'No, I had agreed with Parveen to keep it a secret.'

'How much had Nadeem to do with Parveen?'

'Very little. He was always out in nightclubs and restaurants and taking girls out.'

'When you spoke to Nadeem, what did you talk about?'

'Food mainly.'

'No more questions, Milord.'

'Has any other counsel, representing the other accused, any questions?' asked the judge.

'No, Milord,' replied counsel in turn.

'Now, Mr Beecroft,' said the judge. 'It is for you to cross-examine on behalf of the Crown.'

'Yes, Milord.

'Wahid, had you any part in Parveen retracting her statement?'

'No. I never told her what to say in the witness box. I only told her to tell the truth.'

'Did you ever ring the Sheffield accused?'

'No.'

'Were you ever violent to her?'

'No. I just wanted her to tell the truth. I did tell her to see a solicitor and take advice on her position.'

'Why did she say you'd been violent to her?'

'I don't know.'

'Did your young brother, Abdul, tell you that Asgar had been violent to Parveen?'

'No.'

'Wahid, you knew Asif outside prison in Halifax?'

'Yes, but not very well.'

'How often would you see him?'

'Every week or so.'

'And you were friends?'

'Acquaintances more like.'

'You were a drug dealer?'

'Yes, in a small way.'

'Who sold your drugs for you?'

'Lads in the community.'

'Young boys?'

'No, they were sixteen or so.'

'And you told Asif, in prison, you could make £7,000 a day?'

'No way.'

'Well, you were sentenced to three-and-a-half years in prison for drug dealing.'

'Yes.'

'So you were selling professionally?'

'Yes.'

'When you shared a cell with Asif, what did you talk about?'

'Nothing in particular.'

'Well, you must have talked about your way of life and why you were in prison?'

'A bit.'

'You would talk about things that were on your mind?'

'Yes.'

'You would spend hours and hours together?'

'Yes.'

'And he would talk about things on his mind?'

'A bit.'

'But you say you never mentioned that your sister had married without the family's consent and against its wishes?'

'No.'

'How would Asif know about the drugs in the wall if you hadn't told him?'

'Maybe the police planted them.'

'But you know the officers who conducted the search were independent of the inquiry?'

'So you say.'

'So you believe that the young PC, who was working with another, put the drugs in the wall?'

'I don't know.'

'You know that the prosecution case is that the killers were from Sheffield?'

'So you say.'

'In the dock with you are two white men and an Asian.'

'Yes.'

'How would Asif know that they were alleged to be the killers?'

'I don't know.'

'It's because you told Asif that.'

'No.'

'What would you think of shooting, in cold blood, a man who was kneeling down?'

148

'Terrible.'

'And if he was an Asian like yourself?'

'Terrible.'

'Would you report it to the police if someone told you he had done that?'

'Maybe.'

'No more questions, Milord.'

'Any re-examination, Mr Archbold?'

'No, Milord.'

'Thank you, Mr Mahmood, you may return to the dock,' said the judge.

'Do any of the other defendants wish to give evidence?' asked the judge.

'No,' said counsel for the remaining defendants in turn.

'Have the remaining three defendants been warned that the jury may draw an adverse inference from failure to give evidence?' asked the judge.

'Yes, Milord,' said counsel for the three Sheffield men in turn.

'Very well, we will adjourn at that point until tomorrow morning when counsel will address you.'

Turnbull and Jasper went to the pub.

'Well, that's all the evidence,' said Turnbull. 'I always thought the Sheffield men wouldn't give evidence. What do you think?'

'Let's wait and see what the speeches produce. The fat lady hasn't sung yet. I think we will get a balanced summing up. I think our case is strong. Asif is the only weak link. It's now in the lap of the Gods,' said Jasper.

'I agree,' said Turnbull. 'All we can do now is have a drink and rely on the common sense of the jury.'

Chapter 31
The Summing Up

The following day was taken up with speeches by counsel. Mr Beecroft went first, outlining his case against each defendant in turn.

After lunch came the defence speeches, after which the judge said, 'Tomorrow morning I will sum up. Ten o'clock start please. Members of the jury, you may leave court. Remember my warnings.'

The jury left the courtroom and the judge then retired.

The following morning, Mr Justice Griffiths came into court at 10:00 a.m. to begin his summing up.

'Ladies and gentlemen of the jury, on Sunday the sixth of February, 2005, at just before eight o'clock in the evening, Mahmood Asgar, a young, twenty-nine-year-old man, was shot at almost point blank range in the back. You can hardly imagine a more cowardly killing. The shooting of an unarmed man, in the back, at point-blank range. He survived for several hours, but was pronounced dead at Halifax General Infirmary at four o'clock the following morning. He was, you may think, taken to the scene and executed. These five men in the dock are said, by the prosecution, to be responsible for that execution.

'Nadeem and Wahid, as they have become known, are said to be the recruiters. Leonard, Fazal and Rastrick are said to be the paid executioners. It is our job between us to try these five men in turn.

'You and I have very different functions, as will have become apparent to you during the trial. I am the judge of the law and the procedure, I give rulings on matters of law, but you are the sole judges of the facts. It is for you to decide where the truth lies, who is responsible for this killing.

'It is, therefore, you who must make all decisions of fact. Who is truthful, who is truthful at one point in her or his evidence and at another point untruthful. Whether a witness, who has given an account to the police and then changed it in evidence at this trial, was telling the truth in evidence before you or in what he or she said to the police, or whether that witness can be relied upon at all, or whether you can be certain about some things and not about others.

'These are your functions and not mine, and it follows that if I seem at any stage to express an opinion of my own, if you agree with it, adopt it, not because it is my view, but because it is your view also, but if you disagree with it, reject it. My directions are on matters of law, not in any way on matters of fact. You judge the facts and you alone.

'The first matter of law about which I must direct you is of fundamental importance. Anyone in this country charged with a criminal offence is presumed to be innocent until proved guilty and it follows that where the prosecution bring a charge, they must prove it on the whole of the evidence, which includes such evidence as has been called on behalf of the defence and such evidence as has been put forward in agreed facts.

'Sometimes a prosecution case, for obvious reasons, strengthens during a defendant's evidence, because the defendant is laid bare as a liar. Sometimes the defence evidence weakens or destroys the prosecution case and explains away evidence which otherwise has not been explained.

'Where the evidence in this case of Nadeem and Wahid falls within that broad compass, is a matter entirely for you. The prosecution say they were shown to be liars, their evidence suggesting that they had no idea what was going on was nonsense and their evidence strengthens the prosecution case.

'Say the defence, their evidence was perfectly credible and

they do not have to prove anything, all they gave evidence for was in order to cast doubt upon the prosecution case, but also to persuade you of the truth of what they were saying in the bargain.

'The standard which the prosecution must attain, before you can convict any one of these men, is a high one. The prosecution must make each and every one of you sure of guilt. And so the question which you must ask yourselves, when you retire, in respect of each accused in turn, is "Am I sure upon a calm, quiet, objective view of all the evidence, putting aside all questions of sympathy or bias, that the defendant whose case I am considering is guilty?". If you are sure, you must convict.

'You took an oath at the outset of this case to try these men according to the evidence. You swore on whatever relevant testimony you find binding upon your conscience. Some of you affirmed to try the case according to the evidence.

'That is your duty. If you are sure of guilt, your duty is to convict, irrespective of consequences. They are a matter for me. If you are less than sure of guilt, your duty is to acquit. You cannot fudge it. You must return a separate verdict in respect of each accused. The evidence in respect of each differs, the case against each differs. They are tried together for convenience only. You may therefore be sure of the guilt of one and not another or others. You may be sure they are all not guilty, or you may be sure they are all guilty. It is a matter for you to decide, trying each of these men separately.

'I am now going to have distributed to you some written directions on the law of murder, which I will take you through. I may from time to time add a little as I am going on, but this is your template. This is your working document, which you must use in respect of each accused in turn. Now, see the heading, the names of all the defendants, the Queen against five defendants, directions on law of murder, and you will see my signature at the conclusion.

'You are bound by these directions, you must follow them. If I have got the law wrong, a higher court will put me right. Where they lead you in respect of each defendant is entirely a matter for you.

'Paragraph 1 – The definition of murder – murder is the unlawful killing of another with the intention either to kill or to cause grievous bodily harm. Grievous bodily harm is an old-fashioned phrase from an 1861 Act of Parliament which means really serious injury. You might have thought that before you came to this court, in order to be guilty of murder, one has got to have an intent to kill; not so. If you attack someone with an intention to cause him grievous bodily harm and he dies, you are guilty of murder, because the murderous intent is either to kill or to cause grievous bodily harm.

'So that is the definition of murder set out in paragraph 1, the murderer must have either of those intents.

'Paragraph 2 – Asgar was shot twice in the back, I call him Asgar, I mean no disrespect to him, you know his full name. Asgar was shot twice in the back at point-blank range by someone firing a Baikal, 9mm, self-loading revolver. You will remember the evidence of the expert upon that, no dispute; it is accepted by the defence that that is the gun that was used. A third bullet struck him in the leg, having ricocheted off a nearby wall; that was the reconstruction of the expert and it is not in any way being challenged. So, twice in the back and then for some reason one of the bullets missed, hit the wall, came back and struck him in the leg.

'Paragraph 3 – The two bullets penetrated the back of the chest causing massive bleeding, from which he died a short time later.

'Paragraph 4 – It is accepted by the defence that whoever fired the gun is guilty of Asgar's murder.

'Paragraph 5 – The motive for the murder is alleged to be disapproval by Parveen's family members of her marriage to Asgar.

'Paragraph 6 – Motive is not an ingredient of the offence of murder. It is, however, say the prosecution, a pointer to the identity of the person, or persons, who arranged and recruited the murderer, or murderers, and some defence counsel appear to adopt that position also, but saying that the pointers here are towards Abdul Mahmood, the younger brother, and not to Nadeem or Wahid.

'Paragraph 7 – When a man is murdered, as here, each of those responsible may play a different role.

'Paragraph 8 – Thus a person will be guilty of murder if he recruited the murderer for the express purpose of killing Asgar, or causing him grievous bodily harm, or if he was present at the scene, intending to assist, knowing what was going to happen as defined in paragraphs 9 to 12 hereafter.

'So we come to paragraph 9 – Assistance may be by persuading the victim to leave his house, or by ensuring the victim does not escape while the gunman takes aim and fires, or by providing backup to the gunman. Each of those who played a role, having a joint intent, is guilty of murder, provided he is in it together with the others, or another, as part of a joint plan or agreement.

'Paragraph 10 – the essence of the law of joint responsibility is thus that each defendant who shared the intent to commit the offence of murder, or causing grievous bodily harm, and who took some part in it, however great or small, is also guilty of it because he is a knowing participant in the unlawful joint enterprise. Thus, a person, other than the gunman, is also guilty of the murder if he knew the gunman possessed a gun, which he realised the gunman would, or might, use to shoot Asgar with the intention of killing him or causing him grievous bodily harm.

'So, the gunman is guilty of murder. Those who are present are also guilty if those criteria set out in paragraph 10 are satisfied. If a person with the gunman knew he had a gun and he realised he would, or might, use it to shoot Asgar with the intention of killing him or causing him grievous bodily harm, and took some part in the joint enterprise to kill or cause grievous bodily harm, he is guilty of murder. He may end up with a lesser sentence than the gunman or the same sentence, but that is not a matter for you but for me. What is a matter for you, is whether he falls within that definition set out in paragraph 10.

'Paragraph 11 is also extremely important. Mere presence at the scene, simply being a bystander, is not enough to cause you to bring a verdict of guilty of murder. Thus, if you thought it possible, bearing in mind the burden of proof, as I have defined it to you, that a person present at the scene believed that the plan was only to slap up Asgar, which is the expression which has been used, and not to kill him or cause him grievous bodily harm, and you thought it possible that such a person had no knowledge that the gunman was in possession of a gun, which he might use to kill or cause grievous bodily harm, then such a person is not guilty of murder.

'He might be guilty of another lesser offence, which has not been charged in this case, such as a conspiracy to cause actual bodily harm. But he is not guilty of murder, because the shooting, as you will see in the last paragraph, would be outside the scope of the joint enterprise to which he had agreed.

'Now, two of those who sit in the dock are not alleged to have been present at the scene. We know that Nadeem was out with his girlfriend. Wahid was in prison. The allegation against each of them, however, is that each took a part in the recruitment of the killer, or killers. They are the ones behind all this, say the prosecution. They are the ones with the motive, they are the ones with the connections with Sheffield, they paid the

155

Sheffield men to kill Asgar – that is the prosecution case.

'Now, if you are sure, in respect of either or both, Nadeem or Wahid, as you will see in paragraph 12, that he was a recruiter, such a person will be just as guilty of murder as the person who pulled the trigger. A recruiter cannot say "I was nothing to do with it, because I wasn't there", when he in fact sent along the gunman. Such a person is just as guilty of murder as the gunman.

'But what must be proved against each of those two defendants, Nadeem and Wahid, is participation in the recruitment of the killer or killers, in the knowledge that Asgar was to be shot dead or caused grievous bodily harm by shooting. Recruitment to "slap up" would not be sufficient for the reasons I have mentioned already, it would be totally outside the scope of the joint enterprise. The gunman would be on the frolic of his own, as lawyers sometimes say.

'So that is the law that you must apply. You stick to that, you will get it right, have no fear of that. So, you will say to me, well, what defences are available to the offence of murder which would entitle a verdict of not guilty against any or all of these defendants? Well, first of all, so far as the recruiters are concerned, they can say, and it is a defence to the offence of murder, "I wasn't present at the killing", well, we know that, that is accepted, as I have said, Nadeem was not there, Wahid was in prison. "I am not a recruiter, I had no knowledge that Asgar was to be killed", but in the alternative, it has been argued on behalf of the recruiters, or certainly on behalf of Nadeem, "I didn't recruit anyone to kill or cause grievous bodily harm, only to slap up".

'So, if you disbelieve the primary defence, not a recruiter at all, and you believe he was a recruiter, then you will have to go on to consider the second possibility, that he was a recruiter to slap up, not to kill or cause grievous bodily harm; and if you consider that is right, or may be right, then that too would be a defence, notwithstanding the fact that neither Nadeem nor Wahid have expressly raised such a defence.

'To an extent that applies also to Fazal, because if you decided he was not present at the scene but he did recruit, then you would have to decide whether he recruited to kill or cause grievous bodily harm, if so, guilty; if only to slap up, or possibly only to slap up, not guilty. But again, Fazal's primary defence is, "I wasn't present, I didn't recruit, I had no involvement in this incident whatsoever".

'Now, what about those alleged to be present at the scene, participating in the way I have directed you, but not as a recruiter? That is the three Sheffield men. What defences are available to the Sheffield men? Well, alibi, you know what that means from reading your Agatha Christie, or if you are all too young to have read Agatha Christie, you will have watched it on television. Alibi: "I was elsewhere at the time of the offence". Once alibi has been raised, it is for the prosecution to disprove it, to prove that the defendant was not elsewhere at the time of the offence.

'"I didn't recruit", say the men at Sheffield, "and I am not alleged to be a recruiter", that is conceded by the prosecution, "nor did I participate in the offence as a party to the unlawful joint enterprise to kill or cause grievous bodily harm by shooting", that is the defence run by Fazal and Rastrick. Alternatively, "I was recruited to slap up", and the gunman went beyond the scope of the enterprise in the way in which I have directed you.

'The defence raised by Leonard is different, because he admits that he was present at the scene of the murder. He was caught, you will remember, by the DNA on the cigarette butt. He had a smoke at the scene and threw his cigarette butt down. Whether he would be savvy enough to know, even if being present at the scene of a murder, that he could be detected by the DNA on his cigarette butt is a matter for you to decide, but that is how he was caught and so he was backed into a corner by the police, was he not, saying, "Look, I was present, but I had nothing to do with it."

'No other defence has been raised in this case by anyone, so Leonard's defence is "I was present, but didn't participate, no knowledge that the gunman had a gun, no knowledge that he would or might shoot. It happened out of the blue. I had nothing to do with it".

'Can I tell you what is not a defence? It is not a defence to murder that, through fear of repercussions, you dare not go in the witness box. It may be a reason for not going in the witness box, to which I will turn in due course, but it is not a defence to murder for obvious reasons.

'It does not mean he did not participate in the murder. What it may mean is that by giving evidence, he thinks he will, "grass up" others or drop others in it or, indeed, drop himself in it. But fear of giving evidence is not a defence for obvious common sense reasons.

'Nor would fear have been a defence to murder, of being killed or seriously injured by others if he did not participate in the offence of murder. That is what is known as a defence of duress – that your mind was not with the action because you were not acting as a free spirit. That has not been raised in this case. The only defence for those found to be present is, I direct you, as set out in paragraph 11 of the written directions.

'"I didn't participate, even in a small way, in the unlawful joint enterprise to kill or cause grievous bodily harm by shooting. I did not know that the gunman possessed the gun. I had no knowledge anyone had a gun which might be used to kill or cause grievous bodily harm. I took no part whatsoever".

'The shooter heard, it is said, the names of the Sheffield men being mentioned and where they came from and he decided, off his own bat, to stop the car, or have the car stopped, and get Asgar out and shoot him.

'Now, if that is so, or if it may be so, as I have directed you, Leonard would be not guilty because mere presence would not be enough. But, says the Crown, it would be nonsensical for the person intending to kill Asgar in advance, to take with him a witness who has no knowledge of what is going to happen.

'It is obvious from the outset, says Mr Beecroft, that the plan here was to murder and the Crown say whether or not Leonard was a foot soldier, he is guilty of murder. The fact that he may not be the prime mover does not matter, provided the ingredients of the offence, as I have set out, are proved.

'Now, all parties in this case have exhorted you to use your common sense, your experience of the world. I entirely agree with counsel about that. Between you, you have an enormous experience, you all have experience of the world. You are of different ages, you are from different backgrounds and, in some cases, you are from different cultures. That is why you are here.

'You are here as representatives of society, to bring to the issues in this case your common sense and your judgement, having taken an oath at the outset, to which I have already referred in this summing up, to use your common sense and to try these defendants according to the evidence, not on the basis of prejudice or sympathy.

'My suggested approach to you, and this is entirely a matter for you, but my suggested approach to you is that you start by considering the case against the Sheffield defendants. Whether you adopt that approach is a matter for you, but it seems to me to be sensible. Decide first who you are sure was present at the scene of the murder, consider the case in each of the three Sheffield men in turn and the evidence which you can take into account in the case of each. Decide whether you are satisfied so that you are sure of presence, considering each case separately.

'If you are sure that that defendant, whose case you are considering, was present, decide whether he participated in the offence, intending to play his part in the manner I have described to you already.

'Having reached a decision in respect of each of the Sheffield accused, go on to consider the position of Nadeem and Wahid, the two alleged recruiters. Ask yourselves whether you are sure that Nadeem and Wahid were recruiters in the sense that I have described.

'The Crown say, in respect of each, you can be sure he was behind the killing, he had motive, he had made threats to use paid assassins. No one else had a motive to kill Asgar, certainly not his parents and not a sixteen-year-old boy. Paid assassins outside Halifax were used to kill, so the precise threat which was made to kill, which Parveen told the police about, was carried out.

'Wahid, it is said, admitted to Asif precisely what had happened. Nothing Asif attributes to Wahid, say the prosecution, is inconsistent with what actually did happen. Asif only could have known these things because he was told them. They were not in the public domain before he first reported knowing of them to the police.

'Nadeem and Wahid had contact with each other before the killing and with the assassins, as you can see from the telephone charts. Say the Crown, this attempt to implicate sixteen-year-old Abdul Mahmood, who was not earning wages as a packer until after the murder was committed, is a smokescreen. He might have been sent abroad precisely so that these two brothers can turn the blame on him.

'Say the defence of Nadeem, he, Nadeem, had no interest in Parveen's affairs, he had no motive to kill, he had a life of his own which he was leading, he was busy, got interested in other things than his sister's affairs. He never used violence, as alleged by Parveen to the police, against her.

'Say the defence, he was not present at the scene. There is no connection between him and the murderers, whoever they were. The 2033 number was Abdul's and the probability is, although it is not for the defence to prove it, they say, from looking at the other evidence in the case, the probability is that Abdul is the one who set up others to slap up Asgar, and that went wrong because the gunman, without any knowledge of the others, had a gun on him and pulled it out and shot.

'Nadeem, so it is said, is not proved to have played any part in recruitment, he is not a violent man, he has no propensity for violence. His only conviction was for a minor offence of battery, which I suggest you completely ignore.

'In relation to Wahid's defence, he says "I was in prison. Asif is an opportunist liar upon whom you should not rely". "It is amazing", say the defence, "when the case against Wahid needs bolstering, there comes, out of the woodwork, a cell confession to another prisoner".

'Says Mr Archbold, on his behalf, the telephone evidence is flawed, so many people were using the telephones.

'In respect of either Nadeem or Wahid, taking each in turn, if you consider it is not proved that he was a recruiter and a participant in the way I have directed you, find him not guilty. Only if you are sure that he knew what was to happen, that Asgar was to be shot either fatally or to be caused grievous bodily harm and assisted others to carry it out, could you convict.

'Previous convictions.

'Wahid – we know that at the time of the shooting, Wahid was in prison for offences of supplying drugs to undercover police officers. You had to know that to explain how he came to be in custody and was in a position to make admissions to Asif in the first place. Whether he did or did not is a matter for you.

'Says Mr Archbold, on Wahid's behalf, the convictions for

supplying do not in any way suggest a propensity for violence. On the other hand, say the prosecution, Wahid's conviction for supplying drugs demonstrates a way in which he could have raised money to pay for the killing of Asgar. Asif alleges that Wahid made an admission that as a drug dealer, he was earning five to £7,000 a day.

'The evidence of drugs supply is thus a possible means by which money could be raised. The relevance of Wahid's conviction is, therefore, limited to those two matters: his presence in prison, his potential ability to raise the money. It has no relevance other than that.

'Nadeem has no convictions other than a conviction for battery; that is a minor assault, many years ago. He thus is not demonstrated to have any propensity to commit an offence of the type charged. And I so direct you that you are entitled to take his relatively good character into account in deciding whether he would commit a brutal murder of the type alleged in this case.

'The same applies to Fazal. Fazal has a previous conviction for obtaining by deception and a caution for common assault. He plainly, in the past, has not demonstrated any propensity to commit offences of violence or anything remotely as serious as the type charged. You may think the best thing to do in this case is to ignore those convictions and treat him as a man of relatively good character.

'The situation of Jack Rastrick is different. You have been told, with my permission, after a ruling, that two weeks after this shooting, Rastrick was involved in another shooting in Sheffield. A curry delivery boy was lured to a house under false pretext and shot. Fortunately, he survived to tell the tale.

'Say the Crown, it is almost a complete replica of what happened here. Asgar was lured to the scene and shot, only Asgar did not survive. Rastrick admits he was guilty of that second shooting. He pleaded guilty at Sheffield Crown Court to wounding with intent to cause that delivery boy grievous bodily harm. He pleaded guilty to possessing a prohibited weapon and is serving fourteen years' imprisonment for that offence. You will ask how are we entitled to use that material in the context of this case?

'The answer is this. An important issue between prosecution and defence, is whether Rastrick was present at this shooting on the sixth of February and, if so, for what purpose? The evidence of the shooting two weeks later, to which he has pleaded guilty, says the Crown, demonstrates a propensity to commit offences of the type charged in this case.

'Say the Crown, the evidence of his being involved in the shooting of precisely the same type, with precisely the same type of gun, with precisely the same method of getting the victim to the scene, is evidence which supports other prosecution evidence in this case, that Rastrick was present at the scene of this murder and taking an active part on this occasion, whether as the gunman or otherwise.

'That gives support, say the Crown, to other evidence. His buying of the car with the express purpose of the murder, its subsequent disposal and the telephone contact, the primer on the fluorescent jacket, the admission to Helen Munro, all fit into a pattern, say the prosecution, in establishing that he was not only there at the second shooting with a Baikal 9mm gun, but also on the sixth when, tragically, Asgar was murdered.

'Alternatively, say the Crown, it rebuts the defence put forward to Helen Munro that he was present as the driver, but had no idea a shooting was to take place at all. Rastrick's previous conviction for a second shooting two weeks later cannot, however, of itself, be the basis of convicting Rastrick of this murder.

'If that were the case, you would be convicting, would you not, solely on evidence that he was involved in another offence, and that cannot be fair for obvious reasons. The defence of Rastrick say the second shooting had absolutely nothing to do with this case. Yes, it shows that he was involved two weeks later, but that was an entirely separate offence.

'Convicting him for this murder on the evidence against him, which Mr Mountfield submits is weak, relying principally on admissions to a girlfriend who has an axe to grind and on forensic evidence of gun residue, which is worthless, is unsafe.

'We will now adjourn until ten o'clock tomorrow.'

'All rise,' said the usher. The jury and the judge withdrew.

'Let's get out of here,' said Turnbull to Jasper.

Turnbull and Jasper just escaped the rush hour and were on the M1 in twenty minutes.

'What do you think?' said Jasper.

'We still don't know what Rastrick's defence is. Does he accept presence at the scene or not?'

'Wait for his counsel's final speech. He will conjure something up.'

They drove down into Bradford at about 6:00 p.m....

'We'll meet here tomorrow at eight o'clock and travel together. Have a good evening,' said Turnbull who continued on home.

———————•·••·•———————

Chapter 32
The Trial Continues

The following day, the judge continued with his directions in law. He turned to interviews and the relevance of the caution.

'Before each interview, each defendant was cautioned. If you go to Divider 11, please, you will see an example of the caution at page 1, Nadeem was cautioned at the commencement of the interview in the following terms – "You do not have to say anything but it may harm your defence if you do not mention, when questioned, something which you later rely on in court. Anything you do say may be given in evidence", and Nadeem indicated that he understood what it meant.

'The purpose of this rule is obvious. It is to help prevent defences being raised at the last moment without the prosecution or the co-accused being put on notice of what it is going to be; to prevent an ambush, if you like, that is the thought behind it and why this rule was brought in by an Act of Parliament.

'What the Crown say has happened is that Nadeem has done precisely what he was warned about. "If you do not mention, when questioned, something you later rely on in court, it can harm your defence". Well, he has raised, has he not, various things for the first time when he got into this witness box?

'He said Abdul, his sixteen-year-old brother, admitted to him that he recruited Fazal to hire two men, Rastrick and Leonard, to scare Asgar off because Abdul believed he had struck his sister.

'The basis of that belief is that one day Abdul picked up Parveen from the gym. Parveen's face was red, it looked like someone had hit her. She told him that Asgar had hit her. So, it was said Abdul admitted to Nadeem that he paid Fazal, a man he knew as a doorman in Sheffield through his drug connection, £500 to send someone to slap up Asgar. Abdul made all the arrangements with Fazal.

'Also, it is alleged Abdul sent Leonard and Rastrick to Halifax. Nadeem says "I then spoke to Leonard while he was in custody. He told me he was the driver. Rastrick and Fazal got Asgar out of the house, and because Leonard blurted out Rastrick's name and the fact they came from Sheffield, Rastrick said "Stop the car", got the man out and shot him". Nadeem then spoke to the three men in turn. He asked Rastrick "Where's the gun?" Reply: "Do you want it to be put in the back of your garden?" None of this has been revealed before Nadeem gave evidence.

'My next topic is Asif and how you should approach his evidence. After the murder, on the sixth of February, 2005, Asif claims he overheard conversation between Wahid and Nadeem about what had been seen on television. According to Asif, Wahid said to Nadeem "We should have taken care of her, too". If you are sure he was speaking to Nadeem, that is evidence you can take into account against Nadeem as well as Wahid, but not against the Sheffield men because they were not there to challenge it. Whether you believe Asif's evidence that these things were said is, of course, a matter entirely for you. You saw him, you judge him.

'The prosecution say Asif's evidence is confirmed by other evidences. For example, the evidence of what Parveen said to the police, fits with what Asif says Wahid said to him. It all fits as part of a pattern.

'They say how would Asif know to say to the police the words "Oldham", "Cardiff", "Sheffield", if he had not got them from Wahid? Leonard was not arrested until the seventh of March, 2005. He is the first Sheffield man to be arrested. So, how could Asif know it unless he had been told it by Wahid?

'So, say the prosecution, that is evidence to confirm the accuracy of what Asif was saying. He could not have said these things unless it had come from Wahid and, say the Crown, the cocaine found in the wall confirms the accuracy of Asif's evidence. Thus Asif is reliable, notwithstanding the fact that he is a rogue and notwithstanding the fact that no doubt he seeks to benefit from giving evidence on behalf of the prosecution who say Asif was self-evidently, villain or not, telling the truth. Murder was, even for him, beyond the pale.

'Would Asif put himself at risk if he is not telling the truth? His life, he says, has been made very uncomfortable since it became known that he was to give evidence for the prosecution. Any prisoner would know that, but he has gone ahead without any financial benefit to him.

'Say the defence of Wahid, be very wary of Asif. His black-mail was horrible, extorting money after a bereavement. He is a schemer, an opportunist who is out for no one but himself and this attempt, on his part, to portray himself as having morals and feeling obliged to tell the truth is nauseating hypocrisy.

'Would Wahid say anything, say the defence, to a man he knows to be a rogue and a villain? Asif has a motive to make these things up. He wanted to be moved into Category D in the prison. The police supported his application to move to Category D.

'Say the defence, Asif is a dishonest villain and how convenient for the prosecution it is that this man appears to provide evidence which otherwise, say the defence, would have been lacking against Wahid.

'The method of blackmail, says Mr Archbold, demonstrates a cruelty and a lack of care for his victim that belies his benign exterior. Furthermore, he has been doing it again, says Mr Archbold.

'He made allegations against another man in prison that

he had been writing nasty sexual graffiti against an Asian woman prison officer, which was found by a governor not to be substantiated. Whether it was found to be a lie or not is a different matter, but it was not proved against him and he has been moved back since to a more secure prison.

'So, those are the two positions, in summary form, taken by the Crown and the defence of Wahid. What you make of Asif, at the end of the day, is entirely a matter for you. We'll have a break for fifteen minutes,' said the judge.

The jury and the judge withdrew.

After the break, the judge continued.

'Members of the jury, I turn to the next legal topic.

'The three men from Sheffield have not given evidence. That is something they are perfectly entitled to do. They are entitled to say to the prosecution, "You brought the case, you prove it". The fact that they have not given evidence proves nothing one way or the other. You must not assume anyone is guilty because he has not given evidence. What it does mean, however, is that there is no evidence from the Sheffield accused to explain the prosecution case, which the Crown say points to their guilt.

'A suggestion in a question by counsel, in cross-examination, to a witness is not evidence in the case. Counsel is not in the witness box, the evidence comes from the witness box and the witness may agree with the suggestion, but it is the witness's evidence which matters, not counsel's proposition put to the witness.

'Dealing first of all with Leonard, because he is the one who admits presence, there is no evidence from Leonard as to why he was present or why he was taken along in the first place. There is no evidence from him as to who else was in the car or what he understood the purpose of the trip was.

'There is no evidence from him as to who shot Asgar, why the boot was open, who was wearing the fluorescent jacket, whether he got paid for the trip, whether Asgar was willing to go with them and what pretext was advanced to persuade him to leave the house, who it was who went to the house and knocked on the door and got him to come out, whether he was tricked out, or was forced out.

'If he was forced out, is that why there had to be three people present? And when did Leonard first know the murderer had a gun, and what happened to the gun, and what does he know about the car being burnt out and who did it? And what about the telephone calls that are attributed to his number? No evidence from him to explain the calls.

'All these questions are those which Mr Beecroft said he would like to have asked Sam Leonard if he had made that short journey from the dock into the witness box, but he did not. So his silence may count against him.

'If you draw the conclusion that the reason he has not given evidence is because he has no answer to the prosecution case, or none that would bear examination, you must not convict him wholly, or mainly, on the strength of it, but you may regard it as some support for the prosecution case.

'There is no evidence from Fazal from the witness box to admit or deny his presence. No evidence as to his connection with Abdul, if such existed. No evidence as to whether Fazal accepted money and, if so, to do what? No evidence to explain the telephone calls, why he telephoned 8 Grove Road, Halifax. No evidence as to where he had been with Leonard before he arrived at the Rose and Crown at 10:08 p.m. on the Sunday night, a couple of hours after the murder had been committed.

'No evidence as to who set fire to the car. No evidence as to Sandra Jaimes' assertion that he tried to set up an alibi in advance of the killing. Why did he take the night off on the sixth of February? Did he take the job from Abdul for £500 when the car itself cost three hundred and ten?

'Rastrick has not gone into the witness box to deny the suggestion that he was the gunman or, if not, that he was present and, if so, to say who was the gunman. He has asserted to the police that he was at home, alone, but he has not given evidence to that effect.

'There is no evidence to explain or contradict Helen Munro's evidence. He told her that he had been driven in a car, he was in the back, the car was full of people, two people got out, he heard a shot and only one got back in. No evidence to explain how the gun residue got on his jacket.

'All these are matters which have not been explained or contradicted by evidence from the accused. However, I repeat, none was obliged to give evidence. There is no evidence from the three Sheffield men to undermine, explain or contradict the evidence put before you by the prosecution.

'It is a matter entirely for you. You may conclude that each of them has stayed out of the witness box because he had no answer to the case against him, or you may come to the conclusion that the evidence against him was not strong enough to justify his going into the witness box at all, that there was no case to answer.

'If you come to that conclusion, of course you should not hold his failure to give evidence against him. You should only draw a conclusion against him if you are satisfied so that you are sure that the prosecution case is so strong that it called for an answer and, secondly, that the only sensible explanation from silence is that he has no answer, or has no answer that will stand up to scrutiny.

'Now, the defence say to you, do not draw any inference adverse to each of these defendants in turn from their silence. Of course, it is pointed out that you have five trials going on here. The absence from the witness box of one may be explicable, whereas not of another, or vice-a-versa.

'Fazal, the reason advanced for him not giving evidence was because of fear. The evidence against him, it is said, does not establish guilt. The cell site evidence is equally consistent with his being throughout in Sheffield and moving from one place to another.

'Rastrick, the case is not so strong as others make out. The fact that he bought a car which was burnt out does not indicate he was at the scene. The evidence of others, who may have said he was present at the scene, is not admissible against him. In any event, they all have an axe to grind. Each is saving his own skin.

'The gun residue evidence amounts to nought. There were no stripes on the fluorescent jacket noticed by witnesses. There is no sufficient evidence, says Mr Mountfield, to justify this man going into the witness box at all and even if you do hold it against him, it cannot, in itself, be a basis for convicting.

'Leonard, it is said on his behalf, would be in no better a position in the witness box than he would in the dock because, if he values his life, he could not answer any questions in any case. He is afraid for his family. If you think these amount to reasons why each or any did not go into the witness box, you should not draw any conclusion from their absence from the witness box against them. Otherwise, subject to what I have told you, you may do so.

'The next topic that I have to deal with in law, ladies and gentlemen, is witness statements. I will deal with those tomorrow morning. We will now adjourn. Thank you, members of the jury, you may now retire.

'All rise,' said the usher.

The proceedings concluded.

Turnbull and Jasper left court, missing the rush hour!

'I hope the jury is following all this,' said Turnbull.

'So do I. I think they are, so far,' replied Jasper.

They didn't go for a drink as Jasper wanted to get home early for a change.

The following morning, the judge resumed his summing up.

'Several witnesses have been referred to their witness statements or, indeed, to their interviews with the police, from which the witness statements were culled. This has particularly been so with Parveen who was cross-examined by counsel for the prosecution and for Nadeem and Wahid, at length, as to what she said to the police immediately after her husband's murder.

'The law is that these previous statements from her, whether in interviews or in written form culled from those interviews, are evidence in the case, in the same way as is the oral testimony, which she gave in court. What weight you attach to what she said in interview and what she said in the witness statement, compared with what evidence she gave before you in the witness box, is a matter entirely for you to decide.

'You are the judges of the facts and it is classically your task to take into account the burden of proof, and the standard of proof to which I have referred, to decide where the truth lies.

'It was obvious, was it not, early on in her evidence, from her answers and from her demeanour, that she was hostile to the prosecution in the sense that she was not wishing to give evidence in accordance with what she had said in her interviews to the police and in her witness statement, both of which incriminated her brothers, Nadeem and Wahid.

'Having shown that hostile mind towards the prosecution, I allowed Mr Beecroft to cross-examine her about previous statements she had made, either in interview or in her witness statement. You can act upon those parts of the original interviews and witness statements, providing you are satisfied to the requisite standard that they represent a truthful account and not what she said on the same subject, to the contrary effect, when she got into the witness box in this trial.

'However, I should warn you to approach her evidence with caution. It will be for you to decide if she had any concept whatever of the meaning of the word "truth" and of her obligation to tell the truth, having sworn, as she repeatedly reminded us, to do so on the Koran.

'It will be for you to decide whether she had any impression of the solemnity of this occasion, of the importance of this occasion. Your first impression of her may have been one of considerable sympathy, finding herself between the rock and the hard place, torn between loyalty to her late husband on the one hand and, on the other hand, her two brothers, in whose house she lives with her parents and who stood in the dock.

'She is living in the bosom of her family, is she not now? But, by the end of her evidence, her manner had changed, had it not? Saying, at one stage, in answer to Mr Archbold, that she was bored answering questions about what she had said in interview or in her witness statement.

'You also know that she had been in regular contact with her late husband's family and, notwithstanding police advice to the contrary, she had been in contact with her own brothers. Your overriding impression of his woman may have been that she thinks she knows best about everything.

'Neither the prosecution nor the defence, however, can choose witnesses to events. Witnesses are human beings. They are normal people who can lie, tell the truth, be accurate, be inaccurate, be convinced that their account is accurate when in fact it is mistaken. That is human nature. You do not pick witnesses, ladies and gentlemen, otherwise every witness to a stabbing in the middle of Leeds City Centre would be the Archbishop of Canterbury and the Chief Constable. You do not pick your witnesses.

'Make of this woman what you will. That is why the twelve of you are here, chosen at random as you are, as the best people

173

to decide where the truth lies, using your experience of life as you know it. You saw her, you judge her. You decide which of what she said was true and which was false and how safe is it to rely on her.

'The prosecution say the situation is obvious. She, in the heat and anxiety of the moment, when first interviewed by the police shortly after her husband's murder, without any thought of the consequences of what she was saying, without any chance to fabricate, spoke the truth. Her first reaction was to tell the truth.

'She was so upset that fabrication and the consequences of what she was saying were the furthest things from her mind at that stage. Thereafter, say the Crown, to use an old-fashioned expression, she has been got at. She is between the rock and the hard place. If she acknowledges her original account is true, she will be laying herself open to violence from her brothers, to which she had been subjected when she was younger. She knew what happened to her husband when they defied family wishes.

'She now lives with the very family who she says are behind this killing, so she was driven to say in evidence, according to the prosecution, such things as "I can't remember, I'm confused, I was upset at the time. I never said this. What has been described to me never happened. I never said these things to the social worker, or the family liaison officer, or whoever. It's all lies".

'Well, say the prosecution, the truth is to be found in what she said right after the murder, what she said in interview, what she said in her witness statement and, say the Crown, the truth of what she said is confirmed by other evidence, corroborated by other evidence.

'Saber Malik from Cardiff corroborated her original account to the police. What she said to the family liaison officers corroborated her original account to the police. What she said to Narinda corroborated her account to the police.

'Not so, say the defence, the truth is in fact the complete opposite. When she gave her account in interview, in her witness statement, she had been pressured by her husband's family into believing that Nadeem and Wahid were responsible for the killing which in fact is totally wrong.

'When interviewed, she signed the caution, but it was not an interview she had sworn on the Koran to tell the truth, she was in a hurry to get to her husband's funeral. Her attitude, demonstrated in the interview, did not look like a woman who has suffered great bereavement. The truth lies in what she said in court, which exonerated Nadeem and Wahid from all blame. They were never violent to her, she did not suggest in the witness box they were.

'In the alternative, say the defence, this is a witness with a very complex personality. You must, they submit, be very wary of relying on her as a witness, who is blown off course by any wind which happens to come her way. She exaggerates wildly when it suits her, for her own purposes. She lied about so many things in the course of her evidence. It is simply not safe to reply on a word she says.

'Those are the two positions taken so far as Parveen is concerned. Where the truth lies is a matter for you, bearing in mind the burden and the standard of proof. After the luncheon adjournment, I will turn to summarise the evidence. Quarter past two, ladies and gentlemen, please.'

Turnbull and Jasper went for lunch to a pub that Turnbull knew. It was a short distance from the court and not a jury haunt. Turnbull ordered two pints and some pork pies with mushy peas. They found a quiet corner of the pub in which to enjoy them.

'God knows what the jury will make of that lot,' said Turnbull.

'Well, the judges today are obliged to give all those directions in law,' said Jasper.

'Yes,' said Turnbull. 'When I started in this job, summings up were much simpler. Nowadays, a juror needs to be a member of Mensa to follow it.'

'Yes,' said Jasper. 'But if the judge failed to give any of those directions, his summing up would be appealed.'

'Yes, I agree. His is a difficult job,' said Turnbull. 'And I think his directions in law were very fair. He put the arguments on each side very carefully. After lunch he moves on to summarise evidence. Let's hope he deals with that as fairly. Therein lies our best hope of conviction.'

At 2:00 p.m. they went back to court which re-assembled at 2:15 p.m.

'I now turn to summarise the evidence,' said Mr Justice Griffiths. 'I will draw the strands of the evidence together in chronological order, first for the prosecution, then for the defence. Inevitably, it will be a summary, not a repetition of everything that has been said and if I omit to mention any fact spoken of in evidence which you regard as important, give that evidence, whatever it is, such weight as you think fit.

'Equally, if I mention something you think is unimportant, disregard it, it is your view of the evidence that matters, not mine.

'You will ask why I am obliged to summarise the evidence at all. You have heard it spoken about during the very able submissions from counsel. Unfortunately, I have got to summarise the evidence.

'If I were north of the border in Scotland, I would not have to. But, for reasons best known to someone no doubt brighter than I am, in England, south of the border, I am obliged to summarise the evidence.

'But it may help you to remember things said a long time ago and if I repeat the relevant evidence, just as it came, it will enable you to remind yourselves of various aspects of it which might otherwise have slipped your memory.

'There will not be any more evidence, let me be absolutely clear about that. Each side makes the decision what evidence it is going to call. Each defendant makes a decision what evidence is going to be called on his behalf. So there is no point, after you have retired, sending me a question that cannot be answered by the evidence that has already been given.

'If, of course, during your deliberations, you want assistance as to what evidence has been given and to be reminded of a certain thing that I may have made a note of, and you cannot precisely remember or you disagree between you precisely what was said, then send me a note and I will remind you about the evidence of whatever it is you are in doubt about in order to assist you. I am here to help you throughout.'

Mr Justice Griffiths then began his summary of the evidence given in the trial. At 4:15 p.m. he adjourned for the day, adding that there was a little more for him to say in the morning and then they would be retiring to consider their verdicts.

Court re-assembled at 10:00 a.m. the following morning. Turnbull and Jasper sat patiently. The jury filed in and then the judge, at which point he addressed them.

'You may have heard that, in certain circumstances, I can accept from you a verdict which is not the verdict of you all. Those circumstances have not, as yet, arisen. So, when you retire, you must strive to reach a verdict upon which you are all agreed in respect of each defendant. And, if you have not already done so, please appoint one of your number as your foreman, man or woman, who will chair your deliberations in the jury room and who will answer the court clerk's questions on your return to court as to what your verdicts are.

'If you have any problem during the course of your deliberations, please do not hesitate to call on me, that is one of the reasons I am here. Write it down, give it to the usher and we will sort it out between us, all right?

'Finally, the jury bailiffs will now be sworn. They will be outside your room, not listening to what you are saying, but they will be looking after you whilst you are in the jury room and making sure you do not escape, all right? Yes, thank you.'

The jury bailiffs were duly sworn.

The jury then retired to consider their verdicts and Turnbull and Jasper went to the pub.

The jury retired for three days in all. On the fourth day, they sent a message to the judge that they had reached verdicts upon which they were all agreed.

They filed into court.

The court clerk announced that the jury had been considering their verdicts for thirty hours and three minutes. He then addressed the jury.

'Will the foreman please stand.'

He did so. He was a man in his forties, a bit portly, but smartly dressed in a suit and tie.

The court clerk continued, 'In respect of Nadeem Khan, has the jury reached a verdict upon which you are all agreed?'

'Yes,' replied the foreman.

'Do you find Nadeem Khan guilty or not guilty?'

'Guilty.'

'No!' shouted people in the public gallery.

'In respect of Wahid Mahmood, have you reached a verdict in respect of which you are all agreed?'

'Yes,' replied the foreman.

'Do you find Wahid Mahmood guilty or not guilty?'

'Not guilty.'

'Hurray!' came shouts from the gallery.

'In respect of Sam Leonard, have you reached a verdict in respect of which you are all agreed?'

'Yes,' replied the foreman.

'Do you find Sam Leonard guilty or not guilty?'

'Guilty.'

There was complete silence in the public gallery.

'In respect of Omar Fazal, have you reached a verdict in respect of which you are all agreed?'

'Yes,' replied the foreman.

'Do you find Omar Fazal guilty or not guilty?'

'Guilty.'

Again, silence.

'In respect of Jack Rastrick, have you reached a verdict in respect of which you are all agreed?'

'Yes,' replied the foreman.

'Do you find Jack Rastrick guilty or not guilty?'

'Guilty.'

The judge then directed that Wahid Mahmood be discharged and announced that he would sentence the other four the following day.

The court adjourned.

'Well, that result was much as we expected,' said Turnbull to Jasper as they sat having a coffee in the police room at court.

'The case against Wahid was always the weakest, depending in large measure on the word of a villain. I had hoped that the mention of Sheffield men, before anyone knew about them, and the drugs in the wall would be sufficient corroboration of Asif's account, but we cannot forget that Wahid was in prison at the time of the murder and could do little, if anything, to assist.'

'I agree,' said Jasper. 'Nadeem's case was the second weakest, so we can be pleased that we got a guilty verdict for him.'

Chapter 33
Sentence

The court re-assembled the following morning.

Turnbull knew that when a defendant is convicted after a trial, having denied the offence, no mitigation would be offered on behalf of any of the four convicted men.

Nothing was said on the defendants' behalf after an invitation to do so, by the judge, was declined.

Mr Justice Griffiths asked the four defendants to stand.

The four stood impassively, in the secure dock, flanked by prison officers.

'You four have been convicted of the murder of Mahmood Asgar whose life you took away because he married the woman he loved.

'You, Nadeem, were the prime mover of this offence of murder. You tried, in this trial, to pass the buck to your sixteen-year-old brother, who is somewhere in Pakistan, by blaming him for organizing the murder. I expect he will return when the trial is over.

'You hired the three Sheffield accused, Sam Leonard, Omar Fazal and Jack Rastrick who, for money, carried out the murder on your behalf.

'Were it not for the miracles of science, you four may have got away with it. However, a cigarette butt left by you, Sam Leonard, at the scene, led to your detection.

'I see no reason to distinguish between any of you when it comes to sentence.

'There is only one sentence for murder and that is life imprisonment. I am obliged to state the minimum term you must serve before even being considered for parole.

'That term is thirty years in each of your cases.
'Take them down.'